AURORA STREET

BY: KARLA WILLIAMS NOONAN

Victory Publications

Printed in the United States of America

Cover design by: Jenae Noonan
Edited by: Tiffany Avans

ISBN-13:978-0692840986 (Victory)

ISBN-10:0692840982

To my mother

Introduction

I currently live my life incrementally. My psychiatrist, Doreen says that if I can control small portions of my life, I will eventually be less fearful and control most of my life. Her theory sounds incredibly simple but it has proved challenging to achieve. She wasn't talking about feeling safe and in control for weeks or months at a stretch. No, Doreen suggested that my life increments consist of two hours at a time beginning upon waking and extending every two hours until I retire for the night. I chart my activities and feelings associated with those activities at the end of the two hour increment. If I feel comfortable (e.g. safe and secure in what I'm doing) I can extend the activity for a half hour only. This does two things: 1. I'm reminded that I'm in control. 2. I exercise newly identified coping skills. The process probably sounds crazier than I am, but it works. That's all I care about. It wasn't too long ago that I wasn't even aware of continuous spans of time and because of that and the consequences thereof, I was hospitalized in a mental health facility in which I met Doreen.

Prologue

I am the daughter of a Kansas dirt bowl beauty queen and a poor Colorado oil derrick acrobat. My blood pulsates with the hybrid people of a tri-state area of Smokey Mountains and the ancestor of laundry sweats, icehouse thieves and a smelly cattle rancher. My early childhood memories consist of a small farm town, tobacco spit and basements that smelled of mold and jars of pickles. It was this small town that formed my earliest thoughts and filled my senses which instilled an education that influenced my entire life. While this education proved trustworthy over time, I recall that I instinctively *knew* things before I was

3

three years old that most people never learned in a lifetime. Those "things" may or may not have served me well.

I often think about the town that gave me life and it occurs to me that this small farming town *is* me. The sights, smells, sounds, places and memories comprise every fiber of my existence. And even though I left over sixty years ago, the town continues to exist, breathing in both my conscious and subconscious mind. I frequently close my eyes and mentally walk through the streets recalling the scenes and facades that formed who I am. I am continuously fascinated about the railroad tracks, the post office and the swim hole on the South Platte River. One by one, the endless details of this western farm town connect and continue to breathe life into my flesh and bone.

4

Reminiscing about this town is therapeutic flooding my senses as a tranquil sanctuary against the uncertainty of life. While the memories are usually restorative, there is one particular memory that is unsettling and causes me uncontrolled, pulse pounding anxiety. My maternal grandparents are buried in a cemetery on Aurora Street about one mile from the house on the same street where they lived. The fact that my grandparents are buried on the *same* street as they lived tortures me. Symmetry like this is unnatural, not found in nature and is to be feared.

Session I

"You said something was to be feared.

What frightens you?" Doreen asked while a pencil

is poised on the notepad sitting in her lap ready to

jot down anything significant and diagnostic.

Doreen has short quirky reddish hair that sticks up

and out and I realize that I like it because it is not

symmetrical. She is wearing a western motif blue

denim dress with red beading combined with

expensive Swedish sandals. Her toes are painted in

a complementary shade of red. Odd combination of

dress and shoes, I think. I expected her to wear

cowboy boots with that ensemble. Even though the

Swedish open toed sandals are not appropriate for

that outfit, Doreen still appears well groomed and otherwise "together".

It is our first session and I'm not sure what to expect from her nor do I know what she expects from me. This is dangerous turf and my anxiety is heightened although I'm grateful to be entering my next phase of recovery. I didn't particularly care for the "stabilization" phase because I don't like taking medications. Apparently my preferred herbal remedies were not going to cure this undiagnosed affliction. After several weeks of trial and error with different prescribed concoctions, I have been deemed stable enough to talk with a therapist. Imagine that.

Before meeting with Doreen personally, I saw her in different areas of the hospital interacting with other people. Her demeanor appeared so relaxed and friendly that I didn't immediately realize that she was with her other patients. I saw her walking outside in the garden inspecting the roses and also sitting at tables in the living spaces drinking coffee and talking with other people who looked as relaxed and friendly as she did. I wondered if moving our sessions beyond these four office walls was another anticipatory benchmark in therapy. I daydreamed about conducting psychotherapy in the garden because I think I'd be less anxious than sitting here on the office couch.

"What frightens you?" Doreen asks again using the same intonation as she used the first time she asked it. I mentally return from the garden daydream to this office and this session. I quickly shake my head from side to side in an exercise to change scenes.

"Symmetry," I quickly blurt and without consideration. As soon as I said the word, I began to worry about Doreen's response. I'm smart and aware enough to know that the word 'symmetry' doesn't invoke fear and trembling in the general population. I worry about what she must be thinking. I also worry about myself; how crazy am I?

"Describe symmetry," she instructs. She hasn't written anything on her notepad and I begin to imagine what type of descriptors she would consider note worthy to memorialize. What could I say that she would have to or want to write? The thought of her writing down my words is both exhilarating and frightening at the same time. Doreen tilts her head into my range of vision in an effort to catch my attention. I wonder what she's doing and then I realize that it's a non-verbal prompt to make eye contact with me. I make eye contact, blink and look away.

"Were you far away?" she asks.

"No," I respond. It's not actually a lie. I am physically in the room but my anxiety level is so elevated that I am being overly analytical. Practicing over-analysis is my favorite diversion strategy.

"What were you thinking about?" she asks.

My erratic thoughts resemble ping pong balls bouncing off the interior walls of my brain. Ping. Pong; randomly bouncing here and there over and over again. Pings and pongs are always active. I imagine the bright electrical lights associated with the synaptic process firing on the soft surfaces of my brain. I suddenly recall that Doreen has asked me a question. I'm afraid to tell her that I'm actually engrossed in the process of thinking so I decide on an answer, while true, that won't make me seem like I'm insane.

"I was thinking about what you would write on your notepad. What do you write?" I asked this because I've heard that therapy works better if you're honest with your therapist and my desire is that the therapy works sooner than later.

"Why are you curious about what I would write?" she inquires.

My face flushes hot and I can't determine if I'm angry or embarrassed. I'm beginning to realize that Doreen has a way of rephrasing everything and anything that I say into another question. Talking with her is like playing a game without rules or worse. I panic, thinking that only Doreen knows the rules and that only she has the strategy. The tilting movement of her head occurs again. I make eye contact. I try to recall what she asked and as my throat begins to tighten, I remember the question.

"I am not curious about what you could write," I say harshly because the word 'curious' is not accurately descriptive.

"I am not curious," I say defensively. "'Curious' is not an accurate word. Children are curious. I was thinking about the various possibilities of what you could write and that's different than being curious!"

"How so?" Doreen asks jotting something on her note pad while continuing to look at me.

"What did you write?" I ask excitedly leaning closer to her as if I could read the words on the notepad.

"I wrote 'not descriptive'" she responds.

"Why?"

"'Why' what?" Doreen asks.

"Why did you write that?" I ask.

"I want to remember that you said it," she says.

"Is it important?"

"Everything you say could be very important," she responds laying the pencil in the middle of the notepad. She folds her hands gracefully on top of the notepad.

"Do you recall the first question I asked you today?" Doreen asks.

"No," I sheepishly respond. I sincerely have no idea. It's only about five minutes into the session, but my mind has wandered in and out of

14

time. I've decided that I want to be anywhere but here. This therapy phase in my recovery is not as desirable as I first anticipated.

"I asked what frightened you. Do you remember your answer?" Doreen prompts.

"No," I quietly and shamefully reply.

"It's o.k. if you don't remember, Kay. I'm here to help, remember?" Doreen says kindly. "You said you were afraid of symmetry and I asked you to describe symmetry."

I wondered why she didn't write the word 'symmetry' on her paper instead of 'not descriptive'.

"Kay," Doreen prompts, "Do you frequently get lost in your thoughts?"

I over analyze this question and I'm puzzled about the word choice of "lost". "Define 'lost'," I ask but she doesn't respond. Silent seconds turn into what feels like very long uncomfortable minutes. I wonder why she doesn't respond and define the word for me, and then I look around her office rather than meeting her eyes. Doreen's office is small but comfortable. There's a large window in one wall that frames a flowery tree outside. A couch with pillows sets across from the blue upholstered rocking chair that Doreen favors. Her antique oak desk is located behind her chair. Two of the walls have book cases and in addition to the extensive reading materials are toys and other collectables. A huge overstuffed teddy bear sits on the floor in the corner where the bookcases meet. Three of Doreen's framed credentials hang on the wall over her desk. Next to the couch where I am seated is an end table with a lamp and sitting on it is some sort of green rubbery object resembling a frog. The lamp flickers from time to time and I worry about an electrical short that could ignite the building burning it to the ground after closing. I pick up the green object and determine that it must be an anti -stress toy for moments like these when no one is talking. I squish the frog several times before putting it back in its original place on the end table. I look over at Doreen. She is in the same position with her hands folded in her lap.

"I don't understand the word 'lost'," I say as I remember what she asked before I mentally conducted inventory of her office space.

"I understand that you don't know what 'lost' means. That was my word. Do you have another word to describe your thought processes? I ask you a question and something happens with you. Do you know what that is?" she asked.

"I'm a thoughtful person," I respond while intentionally focusing at the blank wall space over Doreen's head. This field of vision is preferable rather than looking at her face.

"As in 'considerate'?" she asks.

"No," I reply and quickly add, "Yes, I mean, I am considerate but what I mean here is that I think a lot. I'm..." I search for the most representative and accurate word, "analytical".

"Describe your 'analytical' process," she instructs.

I consider the question carefully before replying. If I describe my thought process as ping pong balls misfiring, Doreen may want to prescribe supplemental medication. No more meds.

"Kay," she says, "I asked you to describe

your analytical process. Where are you?"

"What?" I ask.

"You used the word 'analytical'." Doreen prompts.

I decide that I'd better say something because I'm afraid of the consequences if I don't. No more meds.

"My analytical thought process involves considering all of the possible angles," I reply slightly turning my head to see the tree branch tap, tap, tapping at the window which offers me a welcomed and blessed distraction.

"All of the possible angles?" she repeats. "What does this mean?"

I respond to this question quickly. "I like strategy."

"Strategy." She says flatly reaffirming the

word but she doesn't think it significant enough to write it on the notepad.

"Kay," Doreen continues, "At the beginning of the session, I asked you what frightened you and you replied 'symmetry'. We were unable to explore the meaning of symmetry but we did peak into some other possible issues. Our time is up today but I want you to think about what it is about symmetry that frightens you and we'll start with that for tomorrow's session. How do you feel about that?"

"O.k.," I agree straining my neck to look at the clock on the wall behind the couch. The time concerns me. I'm confused about how an hour has passed because it only felt like five minutes to me. I blink a few times to make sure my eyes are working accurately but blinking hasn't altered the fact that an entire hour has elapsed. I quickly shake my head a couple of times to re-orient myself to this time and space.

"I think we made some progress," she states as she rises from the rocking chair, putting her notepad on her desk and opening the door to her waiting room.

"Uh, huh," I stammer as I exit her office thinking about the definition of 'progress'. I wonder, too, if she'll write 'progress' on her notepad after I leave her presence. Doreen shuts the door behind me and as I exit, I replay today's session over and over in my mind. I think that if today's session is an indication, therapy will be a difficult but necessary evil if I ever what to resume a normal life. Although I believe Doreen could be trustworthy, I feel off guard and anxious in her presence because she is a clever and an expert wordsmith who confronts and convicts me with my own words. That's frightening. Suddenly, I feel exhilarated and turn to run back down the hall to Doreen's office to inform her that after just one session, I now understood the rehabilitation process. *My own words reveal mysteries still unknown.* The door to her reception area is closed. The adrenaline from the excitement of my revelation creates ghastly bile that rises in my throat that cannot be contained. Frantically, I lurch forward and vomit into the nearest trash receptacle. I wait a few moments for the next onslaught, but nothing happens. I nervously scan the hall and offices to see if anyone has seen me and I am relieved that no one has. Business continues as usual in this part of the hospital. I covered my mouth with my hand and run back to my room to be sick in private in case there is another episode. I have never been physically ill (except responding to a few mismatched meds) since my arrival and I wonder if this is evidence of Doreen's assessment that progress was made during our session.

After returning to my room, I quietly shut the door and ran straight to the bathroom searching the medicine cabinet for something to clean and refresh my mouth. There is no suitable product so I gargle and spit tap water repeatedly into the sink while trying to resist looking at my reflection in the mirror. In general, I avoid mirrors because I am always shocked at the reflection that stares back at me. But in some mysterious way, the vomiting was somehow cathartic so I felt fortified and sneaked a quick peak at my image while sloshing the refreshing water. The reflective image in the mirror matches my physical image but there is an additional shadowy presence that stands behind me that apparently only I can see. I've seen the presence for most of my life but only became afraid of it after my mother taught me about fear. Today, the shadowy presence is not readily visible and being tired from both the session and being sick, I didn't want to exert the effort to see it. I exited the bathroom needing immediate refuge with my comforter in bed. I slowly climbed into bed, arranged the pillow and pulled the covers over my head. Even though it was only 3:00 p.m., I wanted more than anything to fall into a deep, restful sleep complete with colorful dreams. I felt secure and protected beneath the blankets and closed my eyes in anticipation of sleep. Instead, my thoughts transported me back in time to the town that gave

me life.

The Town

Fort Morgan, Colorado was a fully mature town with a population of 15,671 when I was born in 1952. The cottonwood trees were full, tall and lush and in the late afternoon sun with a gentle breeze the leaves shone and shimmered like jewels. The spring and summer grass grew quickly and smelled and tasted sweet. Flowers in vibrant colors blanketed the landscape everywhere in planned and random gardens. The soil was rich for farming and to this day, I recall the sweet smell of sugar beets and corn coupled with the pungent smell of cattle feedlots. Rain would fall everyday during the spring and summer and occasionally the wind would blow so hard that the neighbors would stand in the alley speculating about a pending tornado and then run to their respective basements as a precaution. Thunder would rattle windows and hailstones as big as baseballs would dent cars and ultimately ruin those lovely flower gardens.

In this small farming community eighty miles northeast of Denver, every home seemed to be located either on the right or wrong side of the railroad tracks. Local conversation was peppered with "north of the railroad tracks" or "near town". "North of the railroad tracks" was the undesirable area of town because of the smaller wood constructed homes, with no garages where large families were crammed into four rooms including the front porch and canning cellar. Located in this same undesirable area was the grain silos, train depot and ice house. The city and county jail was also situated in this area. When one crossed the railroad tracks, there was nothing for miles except an occasional farm or pond.

"Near town", however, described the more exclusive area where churches were constructed on every corner and brick homes sheltered a family with one or two children with enclosed garages and furnished basements. Parks, sidewalks and alleyways were located "near town". It was not surprising that Main Street ran east and west and connected both sides of the town and if there was literally a right or wrong side of the railroad tracks, there was most certainly the right and wrong side of town.

Life in Fort Morgan during 1950 was stable, predictable and reliable. Some called life "boring" there. Watches and clocks could accurately be set with the zephyr train that roared through town in the early morning and late afternoon. Gossip was ignited and passed along clotheslines up and down the alleys resulting from husbands coming home later than usual for the afternoon supper. The obituaries and the crime scenes were the most frequently read and anticipated part of the Times newspaper.

I reflect upon the other poignant details of this town from time to time during moments when I'm conscious and awake. My mother, Peggy and grandmother, Juanita introduced me to Main Street, which included the Cover theatre, JC Penny's and a Drug Store where, as a small child, I would sit at the soda bar and drink coke. There is a rural myth from those days that soda actually contained a small portion of an ingredient known as cocaine. All I remember is that it was a special treat for me to sit on the backless red vinyl bar stool at the counter and drink coke in a tiny class that had been drawn from a machine especially for me. The man who served the drink was also the town pharmacist because he wore black pants and a white short sleeve jacket with a pocket containing pens and a name tag. This man would make a ritual out of serving me the drink. After my mother had lifted me onto the stool, the man would say, "What'll ya have little lady?" I would reply, "A coke, please." I recall feeling very special and grown up sitting at the bar. After the daily soda, my mom, Juanita and I would sit out in front of Penny's on a wooden bench and exchange the latest gossip. Whoever was in town that day was the subject of conversation.

31

Mom and Juanita knew all sorts of things about everybody in town. Mom, Juanita and I would know about things in the town before the daily newspaper could print it. Buying the newspaper and visiting the post office and bank were part of the daily routine. After mom and Juanita read the newspaper, they would assess how accurate the gossip was from the previous day. It was often mom and Juanita's opinion that the newspaper "got it wrong" and that prompted more discussion.

My mother and grandmother indoctrinated me to the civilized part of town, but my father introduced me to other sections that could only be characterized by the locals as the "wrong side" of the tracks. It wasn't unusual that he frequented this part of town because, as a child, he lived there.

Crossing the legendary and forbidden railroad tracks, he took me fishing or to buy beer in a placed called Log Lane. Fort Morgan was considered a "dry" town in those days and one had to buy alcohol outside of the city limits. Log Lane was a place where the houses and buildings were constructed from actual logs and in which was a liquor store I named the "Beer Store". I recall climbing into the 1950 Navy Blue Chevy, which we named "Old Blue" and heading out on a dirt road bumping over the railroad tracks. I stood right next to my dad in the driver's seat with my arm around his neck. He smelled like the combination of sweat and cologne with his curly black hair greased back off his forehead. He often wore tight blue jeans with a white cotton t-shirt with a package of cigarettes rolled into the right sleeve. I remember asking him one day why he kept his cigarettes there. He said that by rolling them into his sleeve, he always knew where his "smokes" were.

Going places with my dad in the car was always a much anticipated adventure no matter where the road led. If he had to stop the car quickly, he'd fling out his right arm to stop me from flying off the seat and into the dashboard. Dad did this, of course to save me from bashing my head but he also used his arm as a restraint because when he was five years old, he flew through the windshield of 1933 car. He and his mother were guests in another family's vehicle when the driver stomped hard onto the brakes. My father flew through the windshield even though he was seated on Lucy's lap. The accident produced a massive forehead wound that required nearly 100 stitches at the local doctor's office. The doctor administered the sutures without anesthetic while Dad was seated, once again, on Lucy's lap. The accident and subsequent treatment for the head wound proved traumatic for dad and so he was particularly careful that I would not repeat history.

We drove over gravel, asphalt and dirt roads. Sometimes we drove where there were no roads; only farmland. Dad would roll up the windows when we drove through the corn fields to avoid flying dirt and other debris from coming inside the car. The interior of the car would become stifling warm during this adventure but the climate only added to the excitement. Other driving adventures often included going to the fishing pond named Muir Springs near the beer store. The fishing ritual wouldn't be complete without stopping at the beer store and buying a six pack of Colorado brew. Locally brewed, after all, was born and canned in Colorado and I recall dad saying that we had to support our own economy. I didn't understand the concept but I knew that in the serious way he said "support our own economy" that it must be very important. So, with six-pack in hand, brown bag lunch and the fishing gear, my dad and I would drive to the local pond in the early morning. "Fish, just like humans, needed to eat early in the morning," Dad explained. In those days, we didn't need to purchase bait because we dug our own worms for the hook. Dad and I would dig into the ground around Muir Springs with our fingers because it was soggy and spongy with green moss. Worms of all sizes were just below the surface green stuff waiting to be plucked and inserted into a glass jar for use later in the day. I learned to bait a hook with a live worm and spit on it for luck. Even though I was very young, I loved to fish and had the patience to sit and wait for the bobbin to tug. Dad liked to cook and eat our catch so using fresh fish as a food source made sense to me even at a tender age. Dad called the fish that I caught "minnows" and told me that they were too small to eat and then he would toss them back into the pond so they could grow up and become a better meal. On the shore of this pond, with fishing gear and Dad's brew, I began my informal education, but there were other things I learned before I was three years old that most people don't learn in a lifetime.

Session II

"Like what?" Doreen asked.

"What?" I asked returning from the extended random day dream and the town's narrative.

"You said that there were other things you learned before you were three years old that most people don't learn in a life time. Can you give me an example of those things?" She asks while shifting her weight in the rocking chair in an effort, I assumed, to become more comfortable. I immediately looked for the notepad but it was not in her lap. An essential element of therapy was missing.

"Where's the notepad?" I lamented rather

than answer her question. I surmised that Doreen anticipated that I will say nothing memorable or noteworthy in this session and this made me feel sad and depressed. I'm demoralized at the onset of the session.

"In the drawer," she replied and then perceptively asked, "What are you feeling right now?"

Recognizing and expressing feelings is also an essential element of therapy and I'm eager to do therapy well.

"I'm sad and depressed," I respond and then I feel immediately feel proud that I have identified two, no three, feelings. I add the word 'proud' to my list of feelings and wait for Doreen's response.

"Identifying three feelings is progress," she affirms. "Why sad and depressed?" she asks.

"I don't know", I said intentionally thoughtful but without significant regard for the question.

"They are your feelings," she says. Suddenly, I feel sadder that she won't let me off the therapeutic hook. Tears pop into my eyes.

"Where do the tears come from?" Doreen asked. Impulsively, I want to scream, "My tear ducts, bitch" but I repress the urge. I feel bombarded with questions I cannot answer. Instead, I reach for a tissue and dab at the moisture in my eyes to bide some time between the onslaughts of questions and answers. As suddenly as the tears appeared, they dried up.

"You identified 'sad' and 'depressed'," Doreen continued impervious to my tears or absence thereof.

"Yes," I respond. Doreen says nothing but tilts her head to make eye contact with me. I think that this particular movement is annoying. It was okay yesterday, but it's already getting old. Why doesn't she just say, "Make eye contact" for God's sake?

"Kay?" she prompts.

"Why don't you just say, 'make eye contact'? " I ask with a dry sarcastic tone. The intensity of the response has surprised even me.

"Why would that be preferable to you?"

"The tilting of your head is ridiculous," I say. "I'm not a child. You can just tell me to make eye contact."

"You feel like a child?" Doreen asks.

"No," I lie.

"You've been talking about an idyllic time

42

of childhood. It sounded lovely," Doreen comments.

"I don't feel like a child," I reiterate harshly.

"Your story didn't appeal to you?" she asks.

'Story' and 'appeal' are the wrong words, I think. Using the word 'story' refers to fiction, and for the most part, my narrative was real. The word 'appeal' is similar to the word 'attractive'. Both words don't describe factual events in my life.

"What are you thinking?" Doreen asks.

"Where's the notepad?" I contentiously ask ignoring Doreen's comment about whether or not my 'story' appealed to me.

"In the drawer," she responds evenly and continues, "Why is the notepad important to you?"

"I don't give a damn about that flipping notepad," I say emphasizing the word 'flipping' like it's as powerful as the other 'f' word. I quickly stand up and try to focus on the door even though it's only about four feet away, but I can't see it. Where's the door? What happened to the door?

"Sit down, Kay," Doreen instructs with a calming gentle voice. I don't sit down but instead turn my head to look at her. She hasn't moved and she appears relaxed and serene. I, on the other hand, am sweating profusely and my heart is pounding erratically like I've just run a marathon. I back away from where I think the door should be. I'm suddenly disoriented and terrified but I continue to backup toward the couch until I fall into the cushion and close my eyes.

"What happened to you?" Doreen asks. "Describe what happened to you."

I tell her about my physiological reaction to

44

her questions about the notepad and the tilting of her head. She seems nonplused.

"You stood up," she prompts. "What's that about?"

"I wanted to escape," I stammer as I grab one of the pillows and hold it close to my chest while feeling like I'm going to faint from the heat.

"Escape what?" Doreen asks as she hands me a water bottle that has miraculously appeared from nowhere. I eagerly drink the water until the bottle is empty and then wipe my mouth with the back of my hand. I toss the bottle into the trash near Doreen's desk. Three points, I think happily. My heart rate is beginning to return to a normal rhythm. I no longer feel hot.

"Escape what?" she reiterates oblivious to my excellent aim and shooting ability with the water bottle landing in the trash can. Even though

some of my body functions are returning to normal,

I suddenly feel small and ashamed. I look at her

face, making eye contact without prompting and

coarsely whisper, "Me; I wanted to escape me."

My Father

My father was also born in the same town as me but in 1928; and his family lived on the "wrong" side of the tracks. Legend has it that his 40 year old mother, Lucy gave birth to my father during her meal break while working in the second story of a laundry. The legendary version is that after giving birth, Lucy cleaned herself, washed the newborn boy and gave him to an older sister to take home and join the other siblings. Lucy immediately, if not sooner, returned to work because she needed the money for that days' work. In those days, wages were earned in a laundry by piecework and the daily wage depended on how many shirts, pants, and assorted linen were washed, ironed and mended.

Giving birth to my father meant that she had one more mouth to feed and more pieces of laundry to service that day. My father was named Charles "Del" Smith and was the 10th of 11 children which meant that Lucy needed regular work to house, clothe and feed her large family. Lucy's husband, Sam, was either in jail or regularly unemployed. Sam drank heavily and consequently was jailed for a variety of offences like drunken disorderly conduct and trapping beavers and muskrats illegally while under the influence. Sam, Lucy and the children lived above the laundry for a while but eventually moved to the end of Duel Street across from the icehouse and next to the railroad tracks. Their home had two small bedrooms and one bathroom in addition to the kitchen and living room that would shake violently with each passing train.

Due to the large age span of siblings, not all of the children lived at home at the same time so there were only two boys and two girls sharing one bedroom sleeping on a huge feather bed. As the children outgrew the bed, they would sleep anywhere they could. Another sister, in her late teens slept in the living room on the "divan" which was also called a "sofa".

The family was poor by any standards but they always scrapped out a living one way or another which often translated into legal or illegal methods of survival. For example, my father was chosen to steal ice because he was so small and could fit through the broken window in the basement of the ice house across the street from the family's home. Ice was a luxury the family couldn't afford to purchase. Dad crawled through the window late into the night and retrieved small chunks of ice and shoved them out to his waiting siblings who were keeping watch with buckets. They'd carry the ice chunks back across the street and put them into their own small icebox. It wasn't unusual for the children to rummage through trash bins behind super markets to scavenge produce that still had some life in it. The soft spots of potatoes could be trimmed off and the remains be used for soup or snacks. Lucy or one of the older sisters would say, "Take an old cold tater and wait," when the children were hungry and waiting for something of more sustenance. Pithy fruits and vegetables were also salvaged for some nutritional "fixin'". In addition to the children whose job it was to rummage trash bins, some of the children would also follow the coal truck waiting for a spill. Coal that fell onto the street was quickly snatched up and carried home to the storage bin. Scavenged coal was often the only heating source during the winter months and the children were "happy" to follow the coal truck making deliveries around town. In the event that coal was scarce the children would "steal" cow chips from the local farmer's field. Cow chips burned as well as coal.

Sam, while often intoxicated, also helped to sustain his growing family. It's important, though, to understand Sam's orientation to this particular society. Sam, it was rumored, was of Cherokee heritage originating from Virginia. This "Cherokee" ethnicity would shadow three generations. It wasn't bad enough in Fort Morgan that the Smiths had a total of 12 children, (11 who survived infancy) and lived on the wrong side of the tracks and were dirt poor, the family was also known as "white trash" and the children labeled "half breeds." Some of the children could pass for "white" because they had a large dose of Lucy's Anglo genes. Some of the children got a large dose of the Native American genes and could only be labeled as they looked: "injun". My father got a large dose of Indian genes thanks to Sam. Dad had black curly hair and dark reddish skin that would get a darker brown during the summer season. Dad could never and would never pass for strictly "white".

Sam, allegedly being Indian, had different cultural and moral values than the written laws of Fort Morgan. For example, trapping and killing animals as a food or clothing source was an acceptable method for an Indian father to provide for a large family. Sam never quite understood why it was illegal to hunt and trap within the city and county limits when the animals didn't observe boundary lines. He killed them wherever he found them. Sam never stopped trapping, though, no matter how many times he ended up in the city jail. Sam would explain to the sheriff why he needed to hunt and trap and the sheriff would continue to explain why it was illegal but this predictable dialog never stopped Sam or the sheriff from doing their respective jobs. When my father was too big to squeeze into the window of the ice house to pilferage he began poaching critters to compensate for the loss of meat and fur resulting from his father's jail time. There is a lingering and persistent rumor that after years of conflict, the sheriff would not lock the cell door so that Sam could leave the jail before dawn to resume his trapping activity. It is also rumored that Sam learned how to drink alcohol excessively in this same jail with this same sheriff. Eventually, Sam would drink with the sheriff while my father went out at night to trap. While the sheriff was involved in drinking with Sam, my father was free to trap without harassment from the law.

Session III

I felt unsettled and anxious since my last session with Doreen because I remembered very little. I wondered if I had been ill or if my medication had a previously undetected side effect that affected reality or memory. Doreen insisted that I attended and participated in each of the scheduled daily appointments but incredulously I have a sketchy memory about those sessions. Doreen assures me that I have been physically in the room with her and responsive to her prompting but I just can't fill in some of the memory gaps. I become frightened when I can't remember specifics. Doreen says that 'forgetting' is a large part of my problem. She reminds me that over the past few weeks we've been talking about my father and his family. That makes me happy because I love and cherish my father and enjoy the stories about his family even though I don't recall relaying them to her.

She spins the rocking chair around toward her desk and takes a calendar out of the drawer. Turning back around, she leans into me and displays the calendar. She points to a particular day and says, "This was the day that you said that you wanted to escape yourself. Do you remember that?" I sit and think for a moment staring at the calendar. Nonsensically, four weeks have elapsed since that session; that is a total of *twenty sessions*. I don't remember much from the past four weeks. I don't remember eating or sleeping. I don't remember conversations with my friends or family.

This experience has happened to me before so I am not entirely shocked but it is the first time that I've been 'caught' at losing time. Even though I'm embarrassed that Doreen has caught me, I am not afraid. I trust Doreen to help me because I sense that no one else can.

"Do you remember wanting to escape yourself?" she asks again as she gently lays the calendar in my lap. I stare at the squares and numbers that represent passing time as something sweeps over me like a cool, invisible breeze and the pressure in my ears stabilize. I shudder.

"What was that?" Doreen asks briefly looking over at the window in her office. It is shut.

"I felt something." I respond.

"What?" she inquires.

"A breeze," I answer carefully. Suddenly,

I'm afraid that Doreen will think I am insane. I imagine the consequences for being insane and I begin to feel excessively anxious and want to run out of the room. I can't be insane. I won't be insane. It is not me who is insane.

"Who is insane?" Doreen asks. At first I think she had read my thoughts and that realization adds to my feelings of panic and paranoia. Then, I realize that I must have said something out loud.

"I'm afraid that I'm insane," I reply as my heart beats wildly and erratically in my chest. There is no rhythm to my fear.

"People who are worried about insanity are too rational to be insane," she says with a genuine smile. My heart rate begins to slow and I exhale and feel briefly relieved at Doreen's words and the fact that I believe her.

"I felt a breeze," I reiterate, listening intently to my own words. Somehow the words are important but I see that Doreen does not have her notepad. I've come full circle back to that damn notepad and the hostility associated with it.

"Where's your notepad?" I ask.

"In the drawer," Doreen responds.

"I know it's in the drawer!" I exclaim loudly. "You always say it's in the drawer!" Now, I am agitated.

"Why is the notepad important to you?" she asks again. Again!

I think before I answer the question. I think about several possible answers but none of them seem sincere. They could be good answers, but I understand that honest answers are better than good answers in therapy. Therapy is not like being in school when good answers are judged the best. Good answers reward you with the highest grades combined with the teacher's praise and attention. I wonder what honest answers get you.

"Kay?" Doreen prompts. I know she is going to ask about my thought processes so I respond before she asks.

"Good answers," I reply.

"Excuse me?" she asks.

"I was thinking about good answers as opposed to honest answers. I know I'm supposed to give you honest answers but I don't know the consequences of providing honest answers. Good answers result in attention and praise and yes, I do like attention and praise." This response comes out in one fluid breath.

"Don't we all like attention and praise?" she

sighs. She laughs and I smile. This could be a sincere moment between us.

"Kay," she says after the smile subsides, "How long are you going to avoid my question about the significance of the notepad?"

"I'm not avoiding you!" I snap. "I'm thinking about my answer."

"I said, 'avoid my question'. I didn't say you were avoiding me, Kay" Doreen clarifies.

"I'm not avoiding the question, either."

Doreen raises her right eyebrow. I've never seen her do this before or at least I don't remember her doing it. I begin to look around the office and decide that I've seen everything and there is nothing of interest anymore. The tree outside the window does not pique my interest. I look at Doreen. She looks at me. I concede that I should answer the question.

"I want you to have the notepad because I want you to write significant and important things in it." I finally say and realize that it's an honest answer. Now I'll have the opportunity to experience the consequences of honesty.

"What kind of significant and important things?" she asks. I'm suddenly angry at the realization that honest responses results in more questions. I should have known this would happen, but I squelch the feelings of anger. Today my anger is incidental compared to the words I need to say and have Doreen hear.

"I want you to write the significant and important things that I say." I say quietly as if the words are fragile and might dissolve and dissipate into the air.

"You want to be significant and important?" she asks.

"Yes," I whisper afraid someone besides Doreen will hear as I lean toward her chair.

"Significant and important as opposed to what?" she asks.

"Invisible," I respond as the tears come in a flood.

"You feel invisible?" Doreen asks handing me a tissue. I can't stop the tears and I can't find my voice. I squeak out a "yes" to her question. Doreen repeats, "Yes?" and I say, "Yes" firmly even though I continue to cry. She waits a few moments and I look at the clock hoping that the session is over but we still have a half hour. I want the session to be over because revealing that I feel invisible makes me fearful like I'm standing on the dark crest of an infinite abyss.

"Do you feel invisible now?" Doreen asks.

"No," I reply and the tears begin to stop. I reach for another tissue as a reserve in case the tears begin again.

"Kay," Doreen begins carefully, "you have done good work here today. You have stayed with me for almost half a session. This is the most time we've been together in one session. Do you realize it?"

"Huh?" I ask since I'm always in the room with her.

"You didn't mentally drift away. You stayed right here in this room with me for thirty minutes." She affirms.

Now, I'm extremely confused as if I wasn't before. I thought honest answers were essential to successful therapy. Doreen is praising me for "staying in the room" with her and not praising my words. I've often wanted to run screaming out of her office in the middle of a session, but I never have.

"What exactly are you talking about?" I ask intentionally emphasizing each word.

"I'm talking about you 'losing time'. This is the first session where you, Kay, have stayed in the session with me."

"As opposed to…." I let my sentence drop off because I am sincerely clueless as I slowly shake my head back and forth. I can't imagine what she is talking about.

"As opposed to emotionally vacating the session," Doreen says.

"What the hell does 'emotionally vacating'

mean?" I ask as I realize that we're actually having a conversation. Doreen isn't rephrasing my words into questions at this particular time.

Doreen explains that during previous sessions I took extreme measures to avoid my responses to her inquiries. She described the many evasive techniques I would employ to avoid revealing meaningful issues to the extent that I had an altered state of consciousness. I was dumbstruck. I was aware that I had been 'losing time' since I was a child but to hear that I was in a state of altered consciousness left me gasping for air and I perceived the room shrinking quickly around me. Black, uneven borders crowded the edges of my vision as I started to slip away.

"Kay," I heard Doreen say, "put your feet flat on the floor and your arms by your side. Look at me. Breathe with me."

I forced my eyes to focus at her and the black started to fade. I continued to feel like a tiny person in an enormous room but the breathing exercise seemed to help. I heard a remote voice resembling my own asking the question that I could not dare: "Who is here if I am not?"

The next thing I'm aware of is that I am in bed in my room. I remember asking, "Who is here if I am not?" but I don't remember the answer and, of course, I don't know how I got into my bed. I quickly look at the clock and breathe a sigh of relief knowing that at most I have lost a few hours instead of weeks or worse. I felt nauseous and also felt that my head was going to explode. I didn't know how to process the information that Doreen revealed in today's session. I carefully recapped the session in spite of a splitting headache:

1. I lost four weeks of time which is the equivalent to 20 sessions with Doreen

2. Some 'other' me attended and participated in those sessions.

I simply cannot internalize what Doreen said. Cognitively, I understand the concept but I can't take it in; but, I realize that the information could be true based on my history of losing time. I pick up the phone and call the nurses station.

"How may I help you?" a woman pleasantly asks.

"Why am I in bed?" Apparently the woman doesn't understand the question because she says, "Someone will be with you in a minute." I hear a click and I return the phone to its base. Within moments of hanging up, Doreen walks into my room. This is the first time I have seen her outside of her office. Alarmed and alert, I sit up straightly in my bed.

"Hello," she says pleasantly. "How are you feeling?"

"Uh, okay," I respond while wondering what crisis has brought her to my room.

We look at each for a few moments without saying words. These quiet moments don't nearly concern me now as much as they did in our earlier sessions. I've learned that silence is not always dangerous. Doreen pulls a chair over closer to my bed and sits down.

"Do you mind?" she asks.

"No, no," I mumble. Finally, I summons enough nerve to ask, "What are you doing here?"

"I've come to see if you are alright. You

had quite a shock today." She says casually.

I defend myself. "I only lost a couple of hours today, " I say hurriedly before she can accuse me of more.

"No, you didn't lose any time," she says much to my surprise.

"Huh?"

"You fainted," Doreen says with a small reassuring smile. Fainting is better than losing time I think and I smile, too.

"What do you remember?" she asks while crossing her legs, then crossing her hands on her knees.

I relax a little and adjust the pillow behind my back before answering. My hands feel awkward so I fold them over my chest. I take a deep breath. "I remember you telling me that another personality is in the room while I am not." It sounds ridiculous.

"That's not exactly what I said. I said that you were in an altered state of consciousness during that time. You surmised that it meant that there was another personality in your place. I didn't say that. Is that why you fainted?" she asked.

"I was overwhelmed and scared," I said.

"That's understandable," Doreen concedes.

The blanket feels itchy and rough on my hands so I move them to my side. I'm not sure how to ask the next question. My fear of being insane returns and as I rehearse several questions in my mind until I realize that there is no sane way to ask what I need to know.

"Who is with you when I am gone?" I ask carefully but the words and my voice sound alien. I can't believe I actually asked that. Dialog from a

1950 black and white sci-fi movie runs through my mind; "Is she alien or human?" some bugged eyed crazed doctor in a white coat asks.

I ask Doreen the same question as before, "Who is with you when I am gone?"

"That's the question," Doreen calmly replies. I'm shocked at her response. I thought she already knew. "You're surprised that I don't know, aren't you?" she asks with a smile.

"Yeah, I am surprised," I admit. "You've been talking with her...him...it?"

"Yes, I talk with her," Doreen says, "but I don't know who she is or if she takes your place. Remember, there may or may not be an 'alter' personality."

"Oh, God," I moan realizing that the hard part of my therapy is just beginning. I pull the covers over my head. I hear Doreen laugh and I pull the covers down off my head curious to discover what has amused her.

"What are you laughing at?" I ask accusatorily.

"You're disappearing again!" she says playfully and then I laugh, too.

"What's wrong with me?" I bravely ask not certain that I'm ready for the answer.

"I'm not sure, yet. I have many pieces of the puzzle, but I don't have all the pieces to construct a meaningful picture." Doreen sounds like a diplomat and I don't like it.

"Am I schizophrenic?" I persist.

"I don't know." She responds.

"You're leaning toward some diagnosis, aren't you?" I ask urgently because I feel like my assertiveness has a limit.

"From what I've observed so far, I believe you have a mild form of Dissociative Identity Disorder," Doreen says.

I quickly push back the covers and swing my feet over to the floor. As I try to stand, I become dizzy and just as quickly sit back on the edge of the bed. Doreen rises to help me from falling forward onto the floor but I tell her that I'm o.k. I sit down on the side of the bed and she sits down on the bed next to me.

"Remember you fainted," she says soothingly. "Don't exert yourself."

"What's 'disassociate identity disorder'?" I ask suddenly very tired. I'm not even sure I want to hear Doreen's answer as I anticipate the amount of therapy required to recover from whatever this is.

"It's a mental process which produces a lack of connection in a person's thoughts, memories, feelings, actions or sense of identity," Doreen explains while looking intently into my eyes. I suddenly recall that the eyes are the windows to the soul. I wonder how many souls Doreen sees in me.

"Kay?" she asks. "Did you hear the definition?"

"Yes, and I heard you say 'mild'. That's good, isn't it?"

"There's no good or bad, here, Kay," she says.

"Mild is better than severe isn't it?" I rephrase the question.

"Definitely," Doreen responds, "In terms of the amount of therapy required."

I swing my legs back onto the bed and lay

back casually watching Doreen who is still seated on my bed. I wonder how losing four weeks of therapy qualifies as 'mild' in her dictionary of mental disorders.

"I lost twenty sessions with you. How can that be 'mild'?" I bravely ask. Doreen rises and returns to the chair, sits and crosses her legs in one fluid motion.

"I believe it's mild because you have not experienced serious dysfunction in any of your work, social and daily activities. No one but you, and of course, me, knew that you 'lost time'. You experienced different states of consciousness, but the continuum of your life continued including the therapeutic process."

"And that's 'mild'?" I sarcastically ask.

"Where does the sarcasm come from?"

Doreen asks.

"I'm a cynic. I don't believe you," I say.

"About what?" she asks.

"That it's 'mild'."

"Remember that I said, 'from what I've seen so far'. We have a lot of work to do," she declares.

I feel admonished and act contrite. "What's next?" I ask as I try to arrange my hair into a tiny, tight knot on the top of my head. I sit up straighter in the bed to fortify myself against the answer to the question.

"We need to discover the circumstances of when this disorder began," Doreen said scratching her heel. I think she's bored or distracted and I frown at the realization.

"You look sad," Doreen observes.

"You look bored," I retort. I wonder where

this hostility originates.

"My heel itched," she smiles and continues, "The answer lies in your past."

"How far back in my past?" I ask.

"You tell me," she responds.

More silence rests between us until I realize that I need to eventually talk about my mother. Just thinking about talking about my mother makes me nauseous. I put my feet under the sheet and adjust the blanket.

"When do we start?" I ask laying my head on the pillow forgetting the bun on my head.

"Tomorrow," Doreen says as she stands to leave the room. "Are you up for a two hour session? We're exploring a critical time in your recovery."

Two hours seemed like a very long and

arduous session and I'm not sure why I agreed to it, but I did. After Doreen left the room, I once again pulled the covers over my head, disarraying the hair bun and desiring the peaceful sleep.

My Mother

My mother, Peggy, was born in 1931 as the first child into an affluent cattle ranching family in Kansas. One of the first tasks the American/German family did upon arrival to the United States was to change their last name to Heider from a well-known albeit notorious "butcher's" name from a World War II concentration camp. The Heider family and extended family of aunts and uncles owned oil and corn fields, private ponds, cattle and horse ranches and settled and populated a small town. Except for the occasional tornado and seasonal harsh dust storm, my mother's life was relatively free from the hardship that my father's family encountered. Still, Peggy's parents wanted a better life for their family and moved to Fort Morgan where her father first worked as a market meat cutter before buying a feedlot and becoming a cattle rancher. My mother's family lived on the right side of the tracks "near town". Their two bedroom home had a red brick façade with one bathroom with a claw foot bathtub, a living room, an eat-in kitchen and an enclosed garage. The laundry room was down in the basement where there were two more sleeping areas for this family of four. Unlike the "half breeds" near the railroad tracks, the members of this family were of pure bred ancestors with blue eyes and blonde hair. The German ethnicity was mixed with a little Irish blood on my maternal grandmother's side but for sake of convenience or bigotry, the Irish side was rarely referenced. My mother and her little sister had blonde hair the color of corn silk and sky blue eyes. They were petit, educated and well mannered. The worst thing my mother ever did was smoke cigarettes in the gymnasium at high school. She never got caught so the smoking habit continued into adulthood. During high school, my mother played drums and other percussion instruments in the band. Mother frequently got the lead roles in the drama productions. One memorable part was that of an angel with a long flowing gown and wings made of bed sheets. She flew across the stage suspended in a wire harness and recited her lines perfectly despite the fear of flying. In 1948, at the age of 17, my mother won the Miss Fort Morgan Beauty Pageant and after receiving her crown and trophy immediately handed both over to her mother for storage in a trunk in the basement. Mom was embarrassed that she had actually won the contest.

While attending high school, mother had a friend who had an older brother named "Del" and by some quirky chance of the cosmos, the two started dating. Credit must be given to both sets of parents because neither opposed the budding relationship during a time when snobbery and discrimination were prevalent. My mother's mother said that dad was a hard worker and attractive. Dad's mother said that my mother was beautiful and would produce beautiful grandchildren. After a brief and socially charged courtship involving both sides of town, my parents eloped, with the approval of both sets of parents, and were married in New Mexico in 1950 where their relationship was consummated on the floor at one of dad's sister's home. While there was a lot of passion throughout the enduring relationship, the marriage began to deteriorate on their honeymoon.

Two years later, I was born to these two mismatched parents from two culturally and socially diverse families from each side of town. My father remained with my mother throughout her labor and delivery; although, it was not a common practice during the mid 20th century to have a husband stay with his wife. Childbirth was strictly woman's work and the man, or husband, usually waited in another room reading, smoking or talking with other prospective fathers. Dad was a trooper right up until the time that he fainted onto the hospital floor. He grabbed the curtain that divided the cubicles and ripped it off its hooks as he went down. Mother was mortified that her privacy had been violated by the torn curtain and was screaming for a partition to restore her modesty. Apparently, she was not concerned about my father's prone condition. The nurse also seemed more concerned with my mother's indignant screaming than any potential injuries to my father, because she immediately carried in a portable room divider and stepped over my father to put it into place. Only after some civility had been restored to my mother's sense of propriety did the nurse think to check my father. Smelling salts quickly revived my father and he continued to be very supportive to my mother for the duration of labor and delivery.

My grandmother, Juanita said that my mother thought that I was a beautiful baby but that she also was frightened from the moment I was born. Juanita said that Mom was spooked because I didn't cry upon birth and that my eyes were large and blue and able to focus. Just to relieve the new mother's anxiety, the doctor and nurses confirmed that it was highly unusual for a term baby to be able to focus their eyes and track at birth. Juanita felt that Mom was overwhelmed with motherhood from this very moment.

Juanita also revealed that Dad thought I was special because, according to Indian folklore, every new baby's blood comprises every past and future generation's ancestry. Dad, as a half breed Indian, didn't think it was unusual for his child to be instantaneously "aware" from birth because he thought everything was possible in the spiritual realm.

So, on the first blizzard of the winter season, I was born into a mumble jumble clash of cultural and spiritual traditions. There are not many stories or recollections of my mother's family's spiritual or religious orientation. My mother often talked about an uncle who was a Methodist preacher but I often got the impression that she viewed religion with disdain. She often referred to Christians as hypocrites and voiced the opinion that religion was a crutch, whatever that meant. Regardless of her opinion, the family would attend church for three holidays: Easter, Thanksgiving and Christmas. These holidays were an excuse to buy seasonal clothing and make an appearance in the sanctuary. Mom and I actually wore wrist length white gloves and hats along with our perky spring dresses to the Easter service. We also celebrated May Day, although not a religious holiday, by putting fresh flowers into tiny baskets and leaving them on the porch of her best friends' homes.

Dad's family, however, was rich with spiritual traditions and because of the Native American heritage did not need the four walls of the sanctuary to worship the Creator. Dad's family worshipped at the altar of nature because the entire universe provided evidence of the Creator. Of course, dad learned and passed on these traditions from his father, Sam.

I recall Grandfather Sam standing in his backyard greeting the eastern morning sun, arms outstretched with dirt from his garden sifting through his hands. He would say, "Today is a good day to die" with all solemnity. I remember asking him, "Are you going to die today?" He responded by telling his two year old granddaughter, "Only the great white spirit knows when the moment of death will be, but if our spirit is aligned with his spirit;

any day will be a good day to die." I understood him and nodded. It made sense. Sam's profound moments of spirituality usually ended before breakfast and after he sat down in his worn overstuffed chair in the corner of the living room. I remember him putting a large wad of "tabbacky" in his mouth and chewing until he spit in a large jar near his chair. It's difficult to understand Sam's words while his jaw is full of "chew" so only part of the conversation makes any sense to me. I can only understand the words in between the spitting and the tearing off a new piece of chew. Regardless, I'm polite and act like I know what Sam has been saying. It's pleasant in the living room as Grandmother Lucy often sings songs from the old days, clapping her hands while Sam encourages me to dance. Lucy sang songs like, "Little Liza Jane" and "Skip to My Lou" while I would twirl around the room like a ballerina. Sam would let me dance on the kitchen table which distressed Lucy. She didn't think it was a good idea for a proper young lady to dance on table tops. I didn't understand why not.

Time spent with my mother's parents was quieter and more refined than the time I spent with Sam and Lucy. Time with the Heiders was structured and organized. Grandmother Heider let me help plant flowers in her garden in the spring. I recall helping her take the trash out to the ash pit in the back yard which was used for burning the garbage. Sam and Lucy were colorful and rambunctious and entertaining. The Heiders were sedate and predictable. Yet, my reoccurring and lifelong dream is about the Heiders.

Session IV

In the middle of the narrative about my mother, Doreen interrupted me and asked, "You have a reoccurring dream? Why haven't you told me this before?"

I think carefully before I answer and then I think some more. Two or three minutes elapse before I admit, "I don't know why I never mentioned it before." I notice that Doreen doesn't have her notepad and as if she reads my mind asks,

"Would you be more comfortable if I got the notepad out of the drawer and put it here in my lap?"

"Don't your other clients appreciate the notepad?" I ask. I'm surprised when Doreen

93

answers my inquiry directly instead of framing another question.

"Some of my other clients react like it's a distraction so I put it away for them. I make notes as soon as they leave my office. I think you're the only client who actually misses it!" She turns the rocker around and opens the top drawer of her desk. Out comes the notepad with the pencil in the middle and she places it in her lap. She retrieves the pencil and is prepared to take notes. I don't know what bothers me more: Doreen with the notepad or without. The notepad bothers me regardless if it's in the draw or on her lap.

"How often do you have this dream?" she asks.

"Two or three times a week at least, "I reply.

"This dream is part of your life!" Doreen

exclaims and then asks, "Why didn't you think to tell me about it?"

"I brush my teeth everyday but don't tell you about that, either, " I respond sounding cocky.

"Are you saying that the dream is unremarkable like brushing your teeth or are you saying something else?"

"The dream is not unremarkable," I say defensively. "It's beautiful and reassuring."

"It's 'reassuring' in what way?" she asks making a note. I don't say anything about the note taking because want to remember my train of thought.

"The dream makes me feel safe, I guess," I surmise listening to my own words and feeling surprised at the word choice. I replay the word 'safe' in my mind where it resonates like a holy, sacred word. Safe.

"The reoccurring dream makes you feel safe?" she asks.

"Yes," I whisper.

"You said that you have this dream two or three times a week?" she inquires.

"Yes," I whisper again.

"Do you have a need to feel safe on a regular basis?"

"Don't we all?" I ask recovering my equilibrium.

"I can only speak for myself. I feel safe unless there's an alarming situation. Are you aware of the fight or flight response?"

"Yes, I know the fight or flight response. What's that got to do with me?" I wonder out loud.

"I don't know," she admits with a small

laugh.

"I asked if you have a need to feel safe on a regular basis. Do you feel safe now?" Doreen asked.

"Yes, no," I reply too quickly. She raises the eyebrow and silence follows. I wonder what she wants me to say.

"Yes, I feel safe now and no, I don't feel safe now."

Doreen says nothing and I wait for a verbal or non verbal cue. There is none.

"I feel safe with you," I continue reflectively, "but at the same time, I'm afraid of what will be revealed in these sessions. The answer to the question is both 'yes' and 'no'." As I concluded my comments, Doreen smiled.

"What are you smiling at?" I ask.

"I'm smiling because you were able to recognize and express two conflicting emotions that you felt simultaneously. Emotionally healthy people are capable of doing that. Congratulations!"

I shake my head in disbelief. Who knew that feeling conflicting emotions at the same time was a symptom of mental health?

The congratulatory mood was short lived.

"Let's think this through," Doreen instructs. "You have a reoccurring dream that you've characterized as making you feel safe. Perhaps the dream symbolizes a need to feel safe."

Her response seems trite and logical not worthy of someone with a PhD in Psychiatry.

"That's it?" I ask.

I'm disappointed. I thought all of the dream's symbols were representative of something complex and wondrous.

"I'm speculating. Think about it for a while. I could be wrong. I'll know more once you tell me about the dream." Doreen concludes.

The Dream

I have a reoccurring dream about the
Heiders who are my maternal grandparents.
Actually, now that I'm thinking about it, it's more
of nightmare than a dream because it involves the
Heider graves at the end of Aurora Street.

I suddenly realize that *this* is the symmetry
to be feared. This is the mystery of the universe
that sneaks up on me in dream-like sequences of
otherwise pleasant sights and smells. There is
something hideous about Aurora Street and the
cemetery at the end of the road which elicits
inexplicable sorrow.

The dream begins as I slam the screen door
of the front porch and walk down the concrete

sidewalks buckled by the roots of old cottonwood trees. I walk, passing familiar sites, until I get to cemetery and arrive at the double headstone joined by a flowerpot. I read their names, "Grant and Juanita" along with requisite birth and death dates. The headstone also memorializes their wedding anniversary date and the enjoining flowerpot is inscribed with "Heider".

As I look up from the headstone and turn ever so slightly to focus on the Aurora Street sign I begin to sweat profusely both in dream and in reality. A sickening nausea follows and I begin to fall to the ground.

Suddenly and predictably, the dream scene changes to Grant and Juanita's kitchen. Grandmother is preparing supper at the stove. In this dream, as was in reality, the kitchen is painted in a glossy lime green and the window over the sink looks out into the rose garden, a hedge and the neighbor's home. The window near the refrigerator looks into the backyard and another garden, the tree swing, alley and the ash pit. The ash pit was a large concrete dome with a smoke stack where trash was burned. Sometimes, in my dream, I am laying on the grass in their backyard watching the burning garbage smoke rise into the sky above the alley. The smoke rises and curls and disappears into the atmosphere. Regardless of the ash pit interlude, the dream always returns to the kitchen and the preparation of the family meal.

My grandmother, Juanita, is standing at the sink. She is not Hispanic, although her name is. Juanita was a very unusual name for an Anglo farm girl born in Kansas in the early 1900s. Her parents named their only daughter after a contemporary song they liked titled "Juanita". Still dreaming, I see Juanita moving gracefully around her kitchen even though she appears matronly considering her age. It's an odd observation because she appears both ageless, yet always matronly.

Juanita wears expensive, clunky black orthopedic shoes resulting from a horrific accident. When she was a younger woman, she and her husband, Grant, took their young daughters to a circus. An elephant went crazy during the show, broke loose from his trainer and destroyed the bleacher in which the family had been sitting. Chunks of steel fell onto my grandmother's foot while her husband and daughters ran screaming from the circus tent. The family escaped but Juanita was left behind lying on the ground with a crushed foot while an elephant was running wild inside the circus tent. The beam on her foot was too heavy to move and she fainted from loss of blood and extreme pain. Fortunately, the elephant didn't step on her body as he ran out of the circus tent to further terrorize the people who thought they were safe outside. Juanita's foot and my mother never completely healed. My mother received no outward injury from the crazed elephant; however, she felt responsible for the elephant going crazy and trampling her mother. Somehow Mother got a guilt wire crossed in her brain that was never straightened out for her entire life. Mom said that it was her fault that Juanita almost lost her foot function because she continued to beg to go to the circus even after her parents repeatedly said, "No". Finally, after sheer exasperation, her father acquiesced and the family went to the circus. As soon as the elephant broke free from his trainer, mother knew that she was to blame. Nothing would alleviate or dull Mother's guilt not even when she consumed *her* mother's pain pills. Juanita needed a daily dose of narcotics for residual and chronic pain and apparently never realized that a pill or two were missing everyday. Juanita also needed the support of the clunky orthopedic shoes in which she walked with a distinctive and pronounced limp. The limp was a daily reminder of my mother's punishment for begging to go to the circus.

Returning to the dream, however, Grandmother's house dress is a nondescript gray with a turquoise flowered print bib apron tied at her thick waist and neck. Predictably, she is vigorously stirring something at the stove resulting in the flopping of her underarm skin. Grandmother's weight didn't distract from her overall beauty. She was the most beautiful woman I had ever known with the clearest, sharpest color of sky blue eyes that always seemed to sparkle with some unspoken secret. She always smelled fresh like her garden flowers.

My grandfather on the other hand, although clean, smelled like the cattle feedlot he managed. He smelled like dirt and other cattle ranch substances. The smell never offended me and I learned to identify his particular scent as the "million dollar smell" because feedlots were big money in those days. Grant has left his dirty cow punching hat and boots on the stoop near the basement stairs. It's the rule of the house that he cannot bring those literally shit kicking boots into the house. In addition to the musty smell of hats and boots, I smell the pot roast and steamed potatoes that my grandmother is cooking. My sense of smell is acute during this dream but I don't ever hear anything. I know my grandparents are talking to each other because their lips are moving but I don't hear them speak. They don't acknowledge that I'm sitting at the table. I'm an invisible guest. They are engrossed in an intimate and routine conversation that only includes the two of them. I wonder if maybe they are eternally in their kitchen and by some dream magic, I visit them. Eventually, Grandmother acknowledges me and serves me a dish of hot food, nods and smiles. She serves my grandfather and then takes her own seat. I don't eat during the dream even though the plate of food sits on the table before me. I am content watching their silent sacred supper ritual in which they eat and smile at each other. Sometimes the dream lasts long enough for me to clear the table, put the perishables back into the refrigerator and do the dishes. I wash and Grandmother dries. I smell the green Palmolive washing liquid and feel the soft water and slippery dishes while looking out at that same garden window that frames pink, yellow and red rose bushes.

Upon awakening from this dream, I always feel relaxed, serene and safe. One time, when I was explaining the frequency of this dream and how I felt upon awakening, a friend told me that it was her opinion that the dream was a hint of what heaven was going to be. According to my friend's theory, heaven could be individualized and be what people desired it to be. She said that as an example, heaven could be the Caribbean for some people or for others, the Alps. She suggested that, when I died, my heaven could be my grandparent's kitchen. It's an interesting theory and when I think about eternity in this kitchen, I feel okay about it. But when I consider that the dream always begins with a walk to the cemetery, I'm scared that it could be a precursor to hell. They lived on the same street that they are buried. No such similar symmetry exists in nature and I'm chilled to the bone.

Session V

"Precursor to hell is a strong sentiment," Doreen observes. At the beginning of the session, she apologized for having a cold. She warns me that she may have to sneeze or blow her nose. "Don't let it bother you," she says as I wonder how sneezing and sniffling could bother me.

"Yeah," is all that I can say. I'm speechless and spent from describing the dream.

"Do you feel safe in your grandparent's kitchen?" she asks.

"Yeah," I reply with a flat affect.

"The dream starts with you walking to the cemetery. Is this right?" she asks rubbing her nose with a tissue.

"Yeah."

"Do you become frightened at the cemetery?"

"Yeah."

"The scene changes to the kitchen where you feel safe again, correct?"

Suddenly, I'm interested in where this conversation is going.

"Yes!" I say with more feeling sitting straighter on the couch.

"What is it about the cemetery on Aurora Street that frightens you?" Doreen asks.

All too quickly, I reply, "I don't know," but on some conscious level I know that just as in a good mystery novel, all the clues are obvious and transparent.

"Where does the dream scene change?" Doreen pursues the issue.

I reflect on the dream sequences and recall, "I become frightened at the headstone, " I confess, "and then the dream scene changes to the kitchen."

"Something begins and ends on Aurora Street is that right? Headstone and kitchen are powerful symbols," Doreen says. I nod. She continues, "The dream scene changes from the cemetery to the kitchen after you collapse at the headstone." Doreen says it as a statement.

The observation is over simplified, I think, compared with and relative to the amount of time I've invested in therapy. I frown.

"What's the frown for?"

"I can't believe that my 'illness' intertwines with 'something begins and ends on Aurora Street'. It sounds so simple, rational and logical," I sigh.

"Parts of psychiatry are just that," she

113

responds. "The dream begins at the Heider headstone and you feel frightened. The dream transfers to their kitchen where, as an invisible guest you feel safe. Does this sound correct?"

"Yes," I agree.

"Yet, this is exactly the symmetry you're afraid of. While the symbolism is becoming useful, the trauma hasn't been discovered." Doreen waits in anticipation of my reply.

I exhale in exhaustion.

"We're not done yet," Doreen says. "In one of our earlier sessions, you said that you were afraid about being invisible, yet in the narrative of your dream, you feel o.k. about being the invisible guest for dinner. What do you think about this?" Doreen asks.

"Besides confused?" I laugh.

"Besides confused," she concedes smiling and then, as in an afterthought, she says, "Do you have conflicting feelings about being invisible?"

The question hits me hard like a slap in the face and my face heats up as if I was actually slapped. After brief consideration, the answer to this question surprises me. I have succeeded in embarrassing myself because I learned something interesting in today's session.

I confess, "I hate and like being invisible."

"How so?" Doreen prompts.

"I hate being invisible to someone that I want to see me," I say.

"Who would that be?" she asks while reaching for the box of tissues and sitting it in her lap. She sneezes and dabs at her nose.

"My mother," I reply hearing my voice as a

115

stranger's.

"And yet it was you who decided on escaping the 'bad mother'. You chose to become invisible to her as a coping mechanism of a small child. It's understandable that as a small child you would want, need and or desire your mother. We all do. Under some circumstances, even adults need their mothers from time to time."

I look at her and consider the words but don't reply.

"Here's what I think," Doreen says, "You chose to become invisible as a survival tool but as a small child you still needed your mother. This dynamic created a significant conflict in your social development which precluded bonding with your mother."

I stare at her and slightly shake my head

from side to side in disbelief. Doreen's
characterization of "significant conflict" seems like
an understatement.

"You're speechless?" she asks.

I nod.

"And?" Doreen continues to dab at the
dribble of her nose.

"And I like being invisible with my mother
when I want to be invisible," I answer quietly.

"Both are true," Doreen says and makes a
note. "Something about the 'bad mother' frightened
you to the extent that you needed to disappear or, in
your words, become invisible to protect yourself.
Does that make sense?"

I nod. Doreen carefully scrutinizes my
demeanor before continuing.

"I think it's interesting, however, that a

small child would have the concept of 'invisible'. Small children around the age of three are concrete thinkers, they can't conceptualize abstracts. You must have been a very smart child."

"I knew a lot of things when I was small," I admitted proudly and perhaps a little too eagerly.

"Like what?" Doreen asked.

Knowledge

For example, *I knew* I was spirit before I had a body although I was not yet cognizant of the word 'spirit'. No one in my family told me that. I was told by some "omnipotent other" one day while I lay in the grass in the backyard of our home. I remember the grass was cool on my back and smelled sweet while the sky was gray with clouds forming for the afternoon rain. The sticky warm air was blowing over my body. As I closed my eyes, I heard the "coo" of the mourning doves, the rattle of a train in the distance and the whip of the sheets blowing on the clothesline. I was aware of my mother unpinning the clothes, folding and placing them carefully into the wicker basket. She was moving quickly and efficiently in anticipation of the pending storm. My senses were flooded with sight, smell and sound when the question formed in my mind with an inaudible voice, "How does it feel to have a body?" The voice seemed familiar and as a result I was not alarmed at hearing this question in my brain. I was too young to form the answer to this philosophical question with words, but *I knew* the answer. Before being contained in this small body, I was a spirit. Simultaneously, I also *knew* that being in this body was a new experience. Prior to hearing the inaudible voice in my head, I would watch the hawk at my grandfather's farm perched high on the telephone pole observing one of the many rodents that lived in the feed bin. As the bird lifted from the perch and swooped down on the scurrying mouse, my stomach would "jump" during the hawk's descent. The feeling was similar to what my stomach felt like while dad was driving in "old Blue" going over the "whoop d-dos" in the road, up and down numerous hills in a row at a ridiculously unsafe speed. My stomach felt like that and I *knew* at the moment when the hawk caught the mouse and flew away, that my spirit also soared at another time. I always *knew* somehow that I existed before occupying this body and I also *knew* that I had occupied another body during another lifetime because of one crystal clear memory.

On yet another day, while lying in the grass, I remember asking my mother, "What happened to Grandmother Smith's black stove?"

"What black stove, honey?" Mother responded looking over the top of the newspaper she was reading while sitting on the back stoop. I remember her vividly like the event was yesterday.

Mother was wearing black pedal pushers, a white button down sweater and black and white oxford shoes with white fold-down top socks with a single yellow daisy near each of the folds. I responded using the limited vocabulary of a three year old, "The black stove with the pipe out the top." I captured my mother's undivided attention. She laid the paper on the stoop, walked down the two steps and kneeled down to my level so we were face to face. "What are you and grandmother doing at the stove?" she asked cautiously.

"We are making popcorn in the pan with a screen on top," I said.

"What does grandmother look like?" she asked.

"She has a long skirt with boots and an apron. She has very long hair up on her head," I replied.

"What are you wearing?" she asked.

"I have a long skirt too but black shoes. I am standing next to her when we make the popcorn."

Mother cautiously replied, "Grandmother Smith never had a stove like that, honey. And you never had clothes like that, either." I remember being both surprised and disappointed at the same time. My mother continued in a thoughtful whisper, "Sometimes people remember things that are from another life." After this declaration, Mother stood up, picked up the newspaper and walked up two steps to resume her research on the town's comings and goings. I nod and this three-year-old child accepts this explanation as a perfectly logical because my father's favorite snack is popcorn. We eat it every night as some sort of intimate family ritual but he uses a different popcorn maker than what I remembered from "another" life. I think that if I liked popcorn then, it's only natural that I like it now. (Many years later as I recall this story, a cool chill permeates my body. It occurs to me that popcorn is still my favorite snack and I eat it everyday as a sacred Eucharist in remembrance to my dead father.) I vividly recall the day that my mother told me that some people have memories from previous lives. Older today, but less wise, I believe that we are all born whole and all-knowing having originated from The One. I also think that it takes a lifetime for us to forget all the preternatural awareness that we are born with.

Our family was not religious and looking back, I realize that we were not particularly spiritual, either. It's remarkable and extraordinary then, that I would have any notion of a spirit and past lives before I was three years old. My early spiritual training occurred while my father and I were at the altar of anthills. I recall lying on my stomach with my chin on my hands in the dirt watching anthills. My dad would also lie on his stomach on the opposite side of the mound. He said, "Everything can be learned about life while watching this anthill. You can learn everything about people, the sun, moon and stars right here." I started to ask him a question but he silenced me with an index finger next to his lips. "We learn by watching and not talking," he said. I remember watching ants for so long that I would fall asleep in the dirt. Later in the day, dad would ask questions about our observations.

"What did the ants take into their home today?" he asked.

"Twigs!" I answered proudly.

"What do you think the ants will do with twigs?" he asked.

"Eat them!" I said.

"What else would an ant do with twigs?" he continued. The question and answer session would enthusiastically continue with no wrong or right answers even as we rode back to our home in Old Blue. As I grew and matured, I realized that the questions posed were actually about the social, transportation and organizational structure of the anthill as it related to we humans. As a result, by the age of four, I understood both the spiritual and earthly realm of life as much as a four year old could. Even now it is sacrilege and forbidden for me to disturb an anthill. Now and then, I still pause at a mound of dirt and wonder about what lesson is being revealed for me today.

There were other things I learned before I was three. I learned I had a good mother and a bad mother. Both, however, were the same person. The good mother would run through sprinklers and talk to me at lunchtime. She would color in coloring books and paint with me. She would get down to my level to talk to me. The bad mother, however, would yell and scream and tell me to go away which I learned to do at a very young age. I didn't want to be around the bad mother. I don't remember the first time the bad mother came out but I don't recall being surprised, either. Becoming frightened of the bad mother, I began a careful observation to be able to predict her arrival. I noticed a direct correlation between the bad mother's craziness and the way she curled her hair. The bad mother would come out when she bobby pinned her hair too tight on top of her head. Mother had beautiful golden blonde hair that fell to her shoulders when she washed and pinned her hair there a lot of tiny curls all over her head. I thought that the pin curls were too tight and somehow turned her into the bad mother. There was a direct correlation between mom's tight pin curls, her brain and crankiness.

My father was often away from the home for weeks at a time working on an oil rig in another state. The job paid good money but resulted in Mom and me being home alone a lot. Mothers in general didn't work outside of the home in those

days so except for the afternoon trip to Main Street
with grandmother, mom and me were alone from
morning until night. Both the good and bad Mother
filled her days with cleaning and caring for me in
one way or the other. I remember her being a very
clean homemaker possibly due to the stern German
upbringing. Mother dusted the furniture twice a day
and ran the sweeper once a day. She mopped the
kitchen, bathroom and service porch floors two or
three times a week or more if the weather was rainy
or snowy. She made the beds and did laundry every
day and even if daddy was away at work, she
always cooked supper for her and me. She drank
beer while ironing and watching t.v. every
afternoon. I would get up from my nap and find her
smoking cigarettes and drinking beer at the ironing
board. It was hard to tell if she liked ironing

because she seemed to be in a rhythm of puffing, swigging and pounding. The good mother would stop what she was doing and ask if I had a good nap and give me a hug a kiss on my forehead. But, if her hair was in pin curls, it was my signal to stay away from the bad mother and stay in my room to play. It only took one or two instances of craziness before I realized to stay away from the bad mother. The bad mother would ignore that I had awoken from my nap and she would continue to iron, smoke and watch television. If I said, "Mommy" to get her attention, she would yell, "What?!" without looking at me. If I said, "Mommy" again, she would scream, "What the hell do you want? Can't you see that I'm ironing?" If I answered that I wanted a drink of water, she would respond with a hiss, "Do it yourself. You may not always have a mother."

That admonition became the bad mother's mantra. Once or twice a week while my mother's hair was in pin curls, I'd depend on the signal of the impending bad mother and stay away from her until the good mother returned. I felt lucky to have any signal or warning of the good mother turning into the bad mother.

I have few memories of Mother enjoying me as a child. I can rationalize now, as an adult, that she probably felt uncomfortable with herself or with her parenting techniques. But as a small child, I only knew that I had two mothers and I needed to stay away from the bad one. When I was older, I confronted my Grandmother Heider with my observation that her daughter and I did not bond as well as we should have. She confirmed that I was an unusual child and she confessed that she and my

131

mother thought I was wise beyond my years beginning at a very young age. She admitted that sometimes my mother was frightened at the things I did or said but Grandmother would qualify her statements admitting that her daughter was "high strung" and had "hypertension".

I came to understand that a mother who was afraid of her child might have a problem bonding with that child. Even though I understood it, the question remained, "How can a child feel connected to anything or anyone without bonding to the primary caregiver?"

Still, as a toddler, I relied on the inaudible voice in my brain regularly because it brought me much comfort and feelings of connectedness. The soothing voice would remind me of how beautiful I was on the inside. The voice said that external beauty fades but that the spirit lives forever. I learned from the voice that I had special gifts and abilities that I would share with the world. At first, the voice would only speak to me if I was in a relaxed state while thinking about nature. Later, the voice would speak if I asked it to and then, eventually, I began to respond out loud. I had been responding out loud to the voice for a couple of days before my mother finally asked who I was talking to. Frightened, I responded, "No one".

She said, "How can you talk to 'no one'? Don't you have to talk to 'some one'?" I recall thinking about her question and thinking, too, that it made sense, but I didn't know the name of the voice in my brain. The name had never been revealed so I stared at her because I was speechless.

"Well?" she prompted. That prompting did

not provide me with the capability to respond and I began to feel nervous and slightly ill.

I was afraid if I did not know how to answer that the bad mother would come out even if her hair was not pinned. Suddenly, I thought of an answer! I said, "I will talk to 'some one'!" The answer was perfect because the good mother nodded and continued finishing her house chores.

I began talking to my fingers the very next day. I personified my ring and pinky fingers. Now I had two "someones" to talk to while I was really responding to the voice in my brain. Of course, the voice in my brain knew who I was really talking to. No puppet or drawing adorned my fingers. I named my ring finger "Judy" and my pinky finger was "Licky". I thought that my fingers needed names to officially be "someone". Both of these new "friends" were on my right hand and I shared

everything with these "friends". While I still didn't

have a name for the voice in my brain, the finger

friends provided a way for me to talk to the

"someone" that mother had suggested. This

situation was mutually beneficial. It kept me out of

trouble for talking to "no one" and I could talk to

my fingers whenever I needed to. I was very proud

when a week later my Mother asked who I was

talking to. I had the honest answer to her question

and enthusiastically responded, "Judy and Licky!"

Apparently, Mother understood the logic in this

response because for a short time she was tolerant

of my finger friends. Not only was she curious

about what I told them, she was also curious about

what they said to me. I never told her that the voice

was really in my brain. She routinely asked, "What

are they saying to you?"

I already learned not to reveal any secrets to the bad or good mother so I stopped talking to my finger friends in front of her. Still, every so often, she would attempt to sneak into my room to see if I was talking to them while playing in my toy box. I learned that the only safe place to talk to my finger friends was in the bathroom. I had privacy behind the closed bathroom door. If I spent too much time in there, my mother would politely knock and ask if I was okay. I would answer that I was okay. Mother would say, "Honey, you've been in there a long time. Are you having problems?" I would answer, "No" as I exited the bathroom. I didn't want to share my special finger friends with anyone and particularly not with my mother. They were mine alone and they could be relied on to appear just when I needed them. The finger friends could be trusted. I heard her one afternoon talking on the phone in the hallway while I was playing in the toy box under my bed. She was telling someone that I talked to my fingers. I heard her question, "Normal? How is that normal?" Then, I heard her say, "Uh, huh," several times in a row and then she hung up. She came to my bedroom and leaned on the doorjamb and just looked at me while I sat in the cedar toy box that my dad had constructed. The first thing I looked for was whether her hair was pinned up or not. Her hair was loose and falling onto her shoulders. The good mother was standing at the bedroom door, although I couldn't be sure if she would stay or inexplicably turn into the bad mother.

"Kay," she said softly and gently, "I don't want you to talk to your fingers anymore. The doctor says you need to play with real children. You need to make friends."

I didn't say anything because I didn't know what "make friends" meant.

"Do you understand?" she asked.

I lied, "Yes, mommy," even though I didn't understand. I returned to playing with my stuffed animals in the toy box. The very next day, a girl about my age came to my house for lunch. Mother told me that I should play with my new friend, Ellen and not Judy and Licky. I smiled. Now I had three "someones" to talk with.

Ellen and I had frequent play dates but I continued to withdraw into a personal world of animated fingers and imagination. Ellen was about the same age as me and she played dolls and other

things well. She couldn't talk as good as me,

though, so she was difficult to communicate with

unlike my fingers and the voice in my brain. The

fingers and the voice in my brain knew and

understood the real me. The voice in my brain

talked to me often said that he/she would always be

there for me and take care of me.

Later, the voice became a presence. I would

feel the presence in quiet moments of the day when

I was alone. The presence was a feeling and I did

not hear any words but the presence made me feel

the same way as the voice. I desired the presence

just as I had wanted more and more of the voice. I

began to seek out moments of quiet and solitude

because the presence filled me with peace and

comfort. My mother noticed that I was becoming

quieter and seeking areas of isolation.

"Are you sick?" she asked.

"No," I answered honestly. "I'm happy".

"What are you happy about?" she asked.

I didn't know the words to express the reason for my happiness partly because I didn't want to reveal that the voice had become a presence. I thought and thought about an answer. Both my father and mother had cautioned me about lying. Lying was one of the worst things a person could do. I contemplated the truth and said, "I'm happy because of the trees and the grass." Mother raised her eyebrow, shook her head and went to the refrigerator for a beer.

More and more, I told my mother what she wanted to hear in fear of the bad mother coming out. The bad mother had been somewhat predictable with the pinning of the hair, but more and more the bad mother was coming out without the reliable warnings. I felt tricked as a result and when I felt tricked, I felt stupid. And I didn't like feeling tricked or stupid. I would cry when I felt tricked and stupid. Mother didn't understand why I was so distraught. She thought I was sick. I thought I was able to predict the arrival of the bad mother and stay out of her way, but I couldn't do it. I had no way of knowing which mother I would be encountering so I learned to stay out of sight and say whatever I thought she wanted to hear. I learned another thing: I learned how to escape to protect myself from the feelings of being tricked and feeling stupid.

The first way I learned to escape was by hiding in my toy box and talking with my finger friends and listening to and feeling the presence. I learned how to shut my bedroom door because this kept the bad and/or good mother away from me until it was time for a meal or take a nap. Alone in my room, I could do anything I wanted even if it meant lying still and listening to the reassuring voice in my brain. At times, I didn't want to come out for food and I would tell my mother that I wasn't hungry. Mother sometimes let me skip lunch, but I always had to eat breakfast and supper. Sometimes I would fall asleep in my toy box and wake up to my mother calling me for dinner. I realized one afternoon that my mother could do whatever *she* wanted while I was playing in my bedroom. When I figured this out, I rationalized that it wasn't the pin curls that made the bad mother come out, it was me. I did it. I made the bad mother.

One cold and windy day in November, I
escaped another way. We had a small Terrier dog
named Sparky. Sparky had a high energy level like
my mother. He was snippy and skittish and
couldn't be trusted, either. One day we became
comrades and escaped the confines of the front yard
together. We walked across the busy street to the
church and climbed the stairs to sit proudly on the
top step. It was my very first adventure without my
father. I sat there, with the dog and watched the
cars go by. I felt accomplished. I had gone
somewhere. Predictably, Mother was not happy.
She ran out of the house yelling both my name and
the dog's. Sparky and I watched her look anxiously
for us in the usual spots in the yard as she ran
anxiously from this bush to that hedge. It didn't

143

occur to me to respond when she called my name. I was engrossed in watching her look for us. Suddenly, she turned around and looked across the street. Even from a distance, I could see her face. She looked happy and almost smiled and after looking both ways, ran across the street to join us. I was afraid of the bad mother when she first approached us but her hair wasn't pinned and she seemed genuinely happy to see us. When she sat down next to us she spoke kindly.

"Honey," she said, "The street is very dangerous for a little girl like you. You are too small for the drivers to see and they could run into you with their cars. The cars would hurt you and Sparky. Do you understand?" she asked.

I understood that the cars were big and moved fast and I understood that we could get hurt but this understanding was tempered with the sheer feeling of exhilaration for physically leaving her behind.

"Yes, mommy, I understand," I said.

"In the future," she said taking my hand, "if you want to come sit on the church steps tell me and I'll help you and Sparky, okay?"

"Yes, mommy," I said as I let go of her hand. I remember walking back home with her but not holding her hand. I was independent and free from her, and I liked the way it felt.

I learned to escape a third way, too. The adventure to the church steps taught me that the good and/or bad mother could follow me and therefore, I really had not really escaped. This third way of escaping was much more efficient and I think the voice told me how to do it although I do not specifically recall the instruction. I would imagine a place different from where I was and go to that place in my mind. The first time I tried it, my bad mother and dad were arguing loudly about the job at the oil rig and money. I was sitting in my toy box and decided to take my mind to Muir Springs and remember every fact about fishing with my dad. But a strange thing happened. When my mind "came back" from remembering Muir Springs, my dad had gone back to his job in the oil fields. I asked mother, "Where's daddy?"

She said, "He went back to New Mexico on Sunday."

"What's today?" I asked.

She said, "Tuesday."

She didn't look shocked or concerned, because she knew that I had just learned the days of the week. Mom didn't know that I had escaped the house and their argument by just thinking about escaping. She didn't know that I had really gone away because I guess my body was still in the house even though my mind was somewhere else.

Missing my dad going back to work made me sad. I wondered how I could have missed our departure ritual if my body could still be seen while my mind was away. I counted on my fingers Sunday, Monday, and Tuesday. Three days. I learned then that wherever I was for three days, I had missed my dad going back to work and that made me very sad, indeed. The sadness of missing my father's departure did not deter me from escaping in the future. Escaping the bad mother was quite frequently the only thing I had control of and wherever I went mentally was better than being physically in the house with her.

Not long after I learned how to escape my mother, I began to see another person besides me in the mirror. At first, the presence was a nondescript shadowy form resembling a human outline. Later, the presence began to take shape in a resemblance to me but not actually me. This person was separate and unfamiliar. When I least expect it, I'd pass by a mirror and observe another looking back at me. It takes my eyes a moment to focus on my actual physical characteristics and somehow I morph into who I am

Session VI

"How old were you when you first saw 'the other girl' in the mirror?" Doreen asked.

"Three, I think," I said.

"Were you frightened?" she asked.

"No, curious I think. I wasn't scared."

"Why weren't you scared? I think I might have been."

"Dunno." I responded and sat quietly with my hands folded in my lap staring at the photo behind Doreen's chair. The black and white photo showed two girls in ski gear looking happily back at the camera. They might have been Doreen's daughters, if she had any children.

"Kay?" Doreen prompted. She only allowed a little time for silence because she didn't want me to lose my train of thought.

"I've always felt familiar with what you would call strange or different things. I only feared my mother." I said.

"Because you couldn't tell which mother you were going to interact with, right?"

"Yes."

"These strange and different things were less scary than your mother?" Doreen asked.

"Yes." I responded.

"Kay, you've never mentioned that your mother hit you or hurt you in any way. Did she?"

"No."

"What was scary about her, then?" Doreen inquired.

"She was unpredictable. I felt stupid and tricked." I said. The answer sounded immature and insane even to my untrained ears.

"What was the worst thing she ever did? Can you remember it?" Doreen asked.

"She screamed and yelled," I said.

"That's the worst?" she asked.

"No, the worst was that she didn't care that I was gone. She was happiest with me shut up in my bedroom." I said.

"You sound sad. Are you sad?" she asked.

"I'm always sad and then some" I truthfully replied.

"There are waking moments that I feel mournful but I'm not aware of what I'm grieving about or for whom," I tell Doreen. "An overwhelming sadness swallows me at dawn. My first waking moment is that I'm missing something or someone significant. Autumn is the time of year when this occurs most often. Well-intentioned and caring friends have told me it's because of the changing of the seasons. Less sunshine they say including leaves turning gold and brown and falling to the ground; dog days of summer, the spirit of summer fading. This theory would be plausible if autumn wasn't my favorite season."

"That was beautiful," Doreen says. "Can you describe any other feelings?"

"Feeling life's changes is a source of both joy and grief simultaneously," I respond. What I don't tell her is that in the clashing of otherwise polarized feelings, I mourn.

"'Life's changes'? Don't you mean seasonal changes?" Doreen astutely asks.

I thought about her question. It's a valid question I concede because my feelings are more related to life than a particular season. How do I tell Doreen that it's possible that I have residual sadness from a another lifetime and by telling her that I go directly into the looney bin? Perhaps, I think that if I died young in a previous lifetime I was born into this life with lingering sadness. I think that's possible. On days like today, I wonder if this life doesn't have enough inexplicable sadness of its own as I close my eyes.

"Kay?" Doreen prompts interrupting my reverie. I open my eyes.

"This narrative is filled with imagery that may be relevant to your condition."

"Like?" I ask.

"Imagery-like voices in your head, imaginary friends, feeling stupid and tricked, not the least of which is the 'other' in the mirror.

That's a lot to work with," she added.

"I'm insane. I knew!" I exclaim.

"You are not insane!" Doreen emphasizes. "I would know," she adds with a smile.

"I'm scared," I admit.

"Of what specifically?" she asks.

"All of it," I respond.

"I said 'specifically'. Pick just one thing you're scared of," she instructs.

"I'm not scared of the voice in my head but I am afraid of what it means in the psychiatric world. I'm afraid of the reason I have the voice in my head."

"What do you think the voice in your head means?" she asks.

"I have no flipping idea," I respond dejectedly.

"I think you do," Doreen admits.

"Am I supposed to feel affirmed in your confidence?" I sarcastically ask.

"Do you feel affirmed?" she asks.

I want to scream and run out of the office until I realize that running and disappearing hasn't served me well in the mental health arena or my life.

"I feel stupid," I admit. "I feel stupid because I don't have an answer to the question." I added my rationale to avoid another of Doreen's questions.

"You *do* have the answer," Doreen confidently says. "I wouldn't ask unless I thought you did."

"What's the question?" I ask shamefully since I don't recall what Doreen asked.

"What do you think the voice in your head means?" she reiterates.

I stare at her, squirm in my seat, sit on my hands, chew my lip and exhale.

"I used to think the Voice was representative of spiritual enlightenment. I thought I was special to have the Voice; that the Voice chose me."

"I'm not denouncing spiritual enlightenment or that a Voice can be an example of that. Spiritual relationships are individual. But, as a therapist, I must interject that a young child of three or four doesn't normally have the brain development to recognize something that is not concrete. I'm not saying that you might have exceeded the range of normal growth and development regarding this issue. It's possible. I think what is more relevant to your diagnosis is that you said the Voice chose you."

"That's what I said," I stated more confused than before because Doreen stated the obvious.

"Why would say that the Voice chose you? I'll give you a hint," Doreen said. "Think like a three year old."

'Think like a three year old', I ruminate and then added my own question, "Why the Voice would choose me?" I exhale and inhale. The office begins to feel extremely warm as I begin to sweat under my clothes. I'm thirsty. Doreen placidly sits across from me waiting for a response. 'Think like a three year old' replays in my head.

"Because my mother didn't choose me," I suddenly blurt without thought.

"Exactly!" Doreen exclaims as she becomes more animated. I'm surprised that what I considered a careless, thoughtless response is the correct response.

"Really?" I ask. I'm incredulous but physiologically I begin to calm down.

"Really," Doreen affirms. "I think that the Voice was one of the first manifestations of the alter," she says. "I don't doubt you were a very smart child and in some ways beyond the range of normal growth and development compared to other children of your age. I believe you remembered whatever the adults in your life told you but I don't believe you had the cognitive construct to accurately categorize that knowledge. You categorized information to serve you in the absence of coping skills or a consistently nurturing mother."

I sat and stared at Doreen as I considered her rationale. The theory sounded true and yet I wasn't exactly comforted by the revelation because I had focused on the words "one of the first manifestations of the alter."

"Kay," Doreen said, "I need to hear more about your family life."

The Phone Call

One day when my dad was home on vacation from the oil field, he answered the ringing telephone. I was standing near his legs and I heard him say, "Oh, I'm so sorry. Yes, of course, I'll tell her." My dad hung up the phone and walked into the kitchen. I followed him closely. He said, "Honey, I have sad news," to my mother who was seated at the kitchen table reading the newspaper.

Mother started screaming, "Not my mother, not my mother!" as she threw the newspaper onto the floor and stood up.

Dad calmly said, "No, not your mother," as he pulled my mother into his chest.

Mother continued screaming, "Not my father, not my father!"

Dad said, "No, not your father. It's about your uncle."

With the same intensity that my mother had screamed "Not my mother" and "Not my father", she screamed, "Oh, God which one?" She asked as she sat down again on the kitchen chair.

Dad told her that it was her Uncle Joe that had died of a massive heart attack. "Joe? Joe?" mother questioned quietly, "How could it be Joe? He is the baby of the family."

I remembered Uncle Joe and he was not a baby so I didn't understand what mother was saying but she was very sad. Even though mother was yelling, she appeared to be the "good" mother so I put my tiny arm around her neck to help her feel better. For the next few days, Mother and Dad talked to each other quietly and there was no

shouting or yelling. Mother and me went to J.C.
Penny's and bought new clothes in dark colors.
Mother told me that I needed to be especially nice
to Grandmother Heider because Uncle Joe was her
baby brother and he had died. I loved Grandmother
Heider more than anyone so I couldn't imagine
being nicer to her than I already was. I didn't
understand "die", either so I asked, "What's die?"

Mother looked seriously at me with pinched
eyebrows and I felt very cold with fear that the bad
mother would come out at this very moment. It had
been several days since the last time the bad mother
had come out and I guessed that she was due to
appear. Much to my surprise, the good mother
stayed. She said, "Hmmmmm," and sat down on a
chair.

"What do you think 'die' means?" she

asked. I had been listening to phone conversations and the talk between my parents and the next door neighbors. I understood bits and pieces of their various conversations but I really didn't get the concept of 'die'. I heard big words like 'funeral' and 'cemetery' that had no meaning. The honest reply to mother's inquiry was that I did not know what 'die' meant.

Mother said, "People are born into this world and at some time their body quits working. Usually it happens when people are very old, but it happened to Uncle Joe's body before he was old. Do you understand?"

I answered, "Yes, Uncle Joe's body quit working. But," I added, "What happens when the body quits working?"

Mother thought carefully and replied, "In

addition to people being born with a body, they are born with a spirit that lives in the body. The body can quit but the spirit escapes and lives on." She looked at my face and looked startled when I smiled. I smiled because finally there was a word for what I had already known: the word was 'spirit'. Suddenly, it all made sense. Spirits live forever and occupy flesh and bone from time to time. As soon as I thought this, however, it occurred to me that I didn't know what happened to the body when it quit working. I asked again, "What happens to the body?"

Mother answered, "The body is put into a wooden box and buried in the ground and then dirt and grass are replaced; then the family puts up a stone marker so they will remember the person who died."

I nodded. It made sense and because I had all the knowledge I needed, I walked away from her to go play in my room.

A few days later, I went with my Mother and dad to the funeral and we all wore our new dark clothing. The funeral took place at the cemetery on Aurora Street. I knew this because I knew where the Heiders lived and the cemetery was down the street from their home. I had seen the street sign often enough. It was a beautiful day at the cemetery so I didn't understand why people were crying and putting fresh colorful flowers on the wooden box. I asked my Dad if I could see inside of the box but he said that Uncle Joe was in the box and that he was dead so I couldn't see. My feet started to hurt inside the new shoes from standing in one spot for a very long time so I let go of my Dad's hand and began to wander through the grass looking at the

trees and all the different rocks with the ABCs on

them. I couldn't read the rocks but I recognized the

alphabet and numbers on them. Some of the rocks

were taller than me and had very big writing on

them. I approached a particular rock and stopped

suddenly. I shook my head as if to clear out a buzz

I couldn't hear. I struggled to string together the

alphabet: B-a-b-y. The word meant nothing to me

but I definitely felt something both strangely

familiar and frightening at the same time. The buzz

in my ears stopped and everything went strangely

silent and I couldn't hear the breeze or the birds or

the cars on the road. I turned to look at my mother

and father and observed that they were hugging

family members around the box. Suddenly, I heard

a loud "pop" and as the pressure equalized the

sounds of the day rushed back into my ears. I
protected my ears from the onslaught of sound
because it seemed that everything had become
louder than a moment ago. The inaudible voice in
my head said, "Welcome back". The voice always
made me feel calm and so I was restored to
equilibrium. I felt my father touch the top of my
head.

"What are you doing?" He asked,

"Reading my ABCs." I said.

"Anything interesting?" he asked.

"Yes," I responded pointing to the *B-a-b-y*
letter by letter on the rock.

"This one is me." I said proudly.

My mother gasped and put her hand over her
mouth as she had joined my father and me at a
headstone.

"What did you say?" she rasped putting her right hand over her heart.

"This is me, mommy" I responded. Mother looked at daddy. Daddy looked at me.

"See?" Mother said to daddy.

"It means nothing", daddy said. "She's confused. We've been here a million times before."

Then dad said to me, "Your name begins with the letter 'K', honey. That's a 'B'.

"No, daddy, this is me," I responded pointing to the ground.

My mother croaked, and Dad looked like someone stabbed his forehead with a long needle.

Later that night while I was lying in bed I heard my parent's whispering in their bedroom across the hall from my bedroom. I quietly got out of bed and tip toed across the hall and lay down on the threshold of their doorway with my pillow and blankey.

"Peggy, just calm down," I heard Dad say. "She's just a bright little girl with a great imagination. She'll be a writer one day." I heard him laugh.

"Del," mother said, "You're not with her every waking moment. You have no idea what she does or who she talks to. I never told you that she has a memory from another lifetime for God's sake."

"Did she say, 'Mommy, I have a memory from another lifetime'?" dad asked.

"No, but the memory she described could have been from another lifetime particularly now that she thinks that baby is her." Mother whispered.

"So, you told her that the memory could

have been from another lifetime, right?" he challenged.

"What was I supposed to say?" she asked.

"I rest my case," dad said, "She got that idea from you. There's no way that a three year old child could have any notion of this life let alone another lifetime." I heard the rustle of the sheets which indicated that he had turned over in the bed.

"How do you explain that she said that the 'baby' was her?" mother continued.

"Go to sleep, Peggy," dad instructed.

"I will not!" she said in her regular voice as the whisper disappeared into the darkness of their bedroom.

"Shhhhh," dad warned and whispered, "How could Kay be that 'baby', Peggy?"

"I don't know but Kay has a memory of her

and your mother popping corn on a stove pipe burner top."

"My mother never had a stove pipe oven," dad said.

"Exactly, Del," mother emphasized. "How could Kay recall something that doesn't exist?"

"Peggy," he said, "This is just plain weird. Go to sleep."

"It's definitely weird but it won't be resolved with your head under the covers. How do you explain that she picked out a baby's headstone out of all of the other headstones?"

"That's easy", Dad said. "We've taken her to cemetery before where she has wandered around. That 'Baby's' headstone is near our families' gravesites. Kay's a smart girl learning her alphabet. There's no metaphysical crap going on here. Don't turn the kid into a whacko, Peggy. She's just smart and you're sensitive and insecure."

When I heard that last statement from my dad I knew my parents were not going to whisper anymore and that they would be using loud regular voices. I also knew that in the morning the bad mother would be back so I tiptoed back across the hall to my bedroom and quietly shut the door behind me and escaped.

Genealogy

After some careful and cautious family research as an adult, I learned that the 'Baby' memorialized on the headstone was born in 1919 to my Smith grandparents. Baby was a beautiful child with dark eyes and black curly mop top hair. She was the 7th of the family's eventual 12 children after Stella, Daisy, Grace, Harvey, Hazel, and Ruth. Baby died shortly after birth from an unknown malady. The family did not have enough money for a proper funeral. It broke Sam and Lucy's hearts to think that little Baby would have to be buried in a communal pauper's grave on the other side of town at the end of Aurora Street. The local mortuary stored Baby's remains for free out of compassion for the poor mixed breed family with more children than they should be allowed to have. As fate would have it, the owner of the mortuary was also a member of the Chamber of Commerce and during a meeting, mentioned the poor Smith family with their baby daughter on ice. The owner of the car dealership, also a chamber member, softened his heart and he agreed that his company would provide Baby with a proper funeral, casket, clothes, flowers and burial plot. Six weeks after she died, Baby was finally laid to rest albeit outside of the Smith family plot. The only thing that was missing from the proper funeral was a headstone but after a small article appeared in the Fort Morgan Times newspaper about a nameless baby in the ground another philanthropist came forward to purchase that.

My parents visited Baby's grave on the

anniversary of her birth because Daddy thought it was too depressing to visit his sister's grave in remembrance of her death. He visited the grave with his family as he was growing up and the tradition continued after he married and had his own child. Baby's profoundly tragic death affected the entire family for years to come. Baby's short life had become a symbol of lost opportunity and hope. The gravesite became a holy sanctuary where individuals in the family would go and pray to Baby in the hope that God would favor her innocent prayers.

Session VII

"Excuse the interruption," Doreen said.

"Huh?" I answered.

"This narrative sounds relatively logical," she said.

"What?" I indignantly responded.

"I'm thinking that your dad might have been right about your mother making a bigger deal of the incident than what was warranted at the cemetery after Uncle Joe's service."

"Huh?" I repeated. I was irritated and I intently stared at her forehead trying to explode her head. My internal hostility frightened me.

"Here's what I think," Doreen said as she rose from her rocking chair and joined me on the couch. She had never done that before and it alarmed me. Was she going to say something terrifying?

"I'm tired." I said standing up from the couch.

"Sit down," she instructed. "You've come a long way in your recovery and I'm not going to let you leave this room either physically or emotionally."

"What are you gonna do?" I hissed. "Put me in a strait jacket?"

"Maybe," she replied. She laughed. I didn't.

I sat back down onto the sofa.

"Let's revisit the cemetery during your great uncle's funeral," she instructed.

I shrugged indifferently with a distinct smirk.

"You're being obstinate," Doreen observed.

I laughed. She didn't. Neither of us said a word for a few minutes until I capitulated and asked, "Why is that day in the cemetery significant?"

Predictably, she said, "You tell me."

I thought back to that day as a small child I wandered around the cemetery during Uncle Joe's funeral looking at the a-b-c's on the rock headstones. Some of the rocks were taller than me. I ran my hand carefully and cautiously over the inscribed names and numbers and felt the cold, hard surfaces. I looked up periodically to make sure I could still see my dad and mother standing over the Joe's wooden box. I didn't want to go too away from them here. The only time I truly wanted to disappear was when my dad was gone and the bad mother was around. Uncle Joe had disappeared into his wooden box but unlike the wooden toy box under my bed at home in which *I* disappeared, his box had a lid.

I remember seeing Baby's headstone and recalled being there previously with my dad. Sometimes our adventures would take us here instead of the beer store or the fishing pond. Dad would lovingly stroke the top of Baby's headstone and recall how he'd never met her. I didn't understand how he could be sad about someone he'd never even met and I recalled asking Dad why he was sad about Baby. He said, "She died before she was your age. She disappeared before I met her."

"And?" Doreen interrupted inquisitively anticipating some break through revelation.

I thought a moment before I asked, "You mean this recollection is why I thought I *was* Baby?" I was thoroughly disgusted and disappointed at the lack of flare in the so-called break through drama.

Doreen laughed before she responded, "Yes and no. The initial trauma is not so easily recognized or recalled. But," she added, "I think you're on to something."

"Lead me through it," I asked.

"O.K.," she acquiesced. "Just this once."

"Here's what I think," she said. "Your recollection is full of imagery; wooden boxes similar to the one at home although the one at home doesn't have a lid. You need to disappear somehow without a lid so at a very young age you emotionally vacate or disappear. Your fantasy is

183

that you're invisible. You previously said that you alternately like and dislike being invisible. What I actually theorize is that when you think you're invisible, an alter identity surfaces. The noises you hear and experience are a precursor to the alter appearing. I am also speculating that the figure in the mirror represents the alter."

"I can see her?" I exclaimed horrified as I minimized all of the other information Doreen revealed. I actually preferred the notion that I had a previous life to seeing an alter. Reincarnation was more acceptable to me than insanity.

"It's possible," Doreen said.

I was deep in thought replaying the script from my recollection when suddenly **I** had a revelation.

"And," I exclaim loudly with enthusiasm,

"Dad said that Baby *disappeared* before he met her!"

"Yes…?" Doreen prompted.

"Disappear!" I repeated. "The word 'disappear' is part of the imagery including the fact that Baby disappeared forever."

"What does it mean?" I asked quietly.

"I don't know, yet, "Doreen admits as she stands and opens the door to her office. "But," she adds, "I'm beginning to think that your mother may have had emotional or mental health issues." It never occurred to me all these years that Mother might have also had a problem. I'm genuinely surprised at the notion.

"We'll talk about that theory next time," Doreen says and adds, "and good work," as I walk out the door down the hall to my room. I turn around to see if she's still standing there but the

door to office is already shut.

Session VII

"Where did you go?" Doreen asked.

"What?" I asked absentmindedly.

"You look like you vacated the room. Where did you go?" She repeated.

"Now?" I asked.

"Yes now. You were not in the room emotionally," Doreen stated.

"I didn't know that I left," I said quietly.

"Perhaps this is an example of how you used to escape as a child," she suggested. "What were you thinking about?"

I looked beyond her face to the window behind her chair. It was a lovely fall day and I could see the brown and gold leaves blowing in the wind. The office was chilly and I wished I had brought a sweater.

"I don't remember thinking," I said. "I remember the feeling of the wind on the hairs on my arms."

"Do you know what time it is?" Doreen asked.

"No," I admitted somewhat sadly.

"It's 2:35 p.m. Do you remember what we were talking about when you first came into my office?"

I was surprised that 35 minutes had passed. The fact that I continuously "lost time" amazes me even though it was a common and regular occurrence. Doreen used the term "lost time" for what I referred to as "escaping" when I was a child. There was always enough of me that remained to go through the motions of my life even when I escaped or lost time. No one else except my mother seemed to notice that I had mastered the "art" of escaping. Mother knew my secret or thought she did. She always thought that I was strange. I knew that I escaped but whenever I "came back" I was disoriented for some time. My life's story lacked continuum and context like someone had ripped pages from a book. My memory of the lost time was gone, too. Whatever occurred while I was 'gone' was forever lost. I didn't remember visiting relatives. I didn't remember where I had gotten toys or who had given them to me. I didn't remember haircuts. The list of lost memories was exhaustive and as I grew up the situation would become embarrassing. I would not remember the simplest things like lunch from the previous day.

"Kay?" Doreen prompted. "Do you

remember what we were talking about when you first entered my office?"

"I remember telling you about the dream in my grandparent's kitchen again," I said attempting to focus on her face.

"You have told me about this dream before. Why was it important to tell me again?" Doreen asked. "Did any details in the dream change?"

"No, not really."

"What does 'no, not really' mean? Is 'no' an absolute or are you qualifying your answer?" Doreen asked.

I hated these sessions because Doreen asked questions that were very difficult to answer. If I thought about my answer for too a long of a time, she thought that I was hiding a feeling or evading the question. The sky was darkening outside the window and I wondered about the location of my umbrella.

"Kay?" Doreen asked as she moved her head so that my eyes would engage hers.

"The dream did not change. Every detail was the same. I thought you said that the more I talked about the dream, the less I would be having the dream." I challenged.

"Would you like to have the dream less often?" Doreen asked.

"No, not really," I said. "I like being in my grandparent's kitchen. I don't have a problem with the dream, you do."

"I didn't ask you about the dream and I don't have a feeling one way or the other about it. When you come into the office, I say, 'what are you bringing in today?' and you decide what to begin with. Today, you began with the dream and then emotionally left the room for 35 minutes. Why do you think that happened?" Doreen asked writing on her notepad in her lap.

"What did you write?" I asked.

"I wrote the last part of my question to pair up with your response."

"I was talking about the kitchen and then, I think I actually went there mentally," I said. "What happens to me when you think that I've emotionally left the room?" It was the first time that I was brave enough to ask her. I had only been seeing Doreen for about six sessions and I wasn't sure she could be trusted. I learned a very long time ago not to trust anyone.

"You continue to answer questions but it seems like you're vacant or like you're not fully present in the room. You began talking about the dream but you drifted into the reflection in the mirror and I did not redirect you back to the dream. I'm not sure how the dream and the reflection in the mirror are related, but somewhere deep in your subconscious mind there is a connection. You were talking about your grandmother making the supper as you have before. You seemed like another person while you talked about that. Are you?" Doreen asked.

"What-are-you-talking-about?" I asked emphasizing every word. "What does that mean? Do you think I'm a split personality or something?"

"I didn't say that. Are you concerned that you're a split personality?"

Talking with Doreen was like riding on a merry go round. The conversation always circled back around to me. The sessions left me exhausted, frequently hostile and dizzy.

"I told you about the dream because I had it again last night, but I like the dream. I don't know why I continue to have it night after night. No one else I know has a reoccurring dream like this. That bothers me. What am I saying!?" I asked abruptly.

"I think it's interesting that we made some headway about the Baby issue and yet, we're back to the dream sequence." Doreen said. "In addition, I had planned to follow up on some of your mother's issues in this session and yet, you want to discuss the dream."

"I feel safe in my grandparent's kitchen. I've said that before."

"We've talked about Baby, your grandparent's kitchen, escaping and the bad mother. We haven't explored the possibility that your mother might have had emotional issues that affected your relationship with her." Doreen summarized.

I saw the rain spotting the window beyond Doreen's head and remained mute.

I glanced at a framed photo on the wall behind Doreen's desk and squint to get a better look at something beyond my comprehension.

"What are you trying to see?" Doreen asks swiveling her rocking chair to guess what I'm looking at.

"There's a shadow. I can't see it." I whisper.

"Is there another face reflected in the glass

that you see besides yourself?" Doreen ventures.

"Yes," I hoarsely whisper. I'm frightened beyond control and I hear the whizzing sound and feel the periphery beyond my focus start to go gray.

"Kay!" Doreen shouts.

"What?" I also shout blinking my eyes and training my focus on Doreen.

"Where are you?" She asks.

I am cold, shaking and feel like I have no substance under my skin but as I look around the office I realize I'm still sitting on the couch across from Doreen's chair. My lips and throat are parched.

"Water," I croak.

Doreen magically makes a water bottle appear, unscrews the top and hands it over to me. I gulp it down.

"Where did you go?" Doreen persists.

"I didn't go anywhere," I say incredulously. "I tried to escape but I didn't."

"Why didn't you?"

"You called my name." I admit.

"What were you feeling before you began to escape?" Doreen asks.

"Fear," I admit.

"Of what?" she predictably asks.

"Me," I say. "I'm afraid of me."

"What is it about yourself that frightens you?"

"I see someone in addition to me reflected in glass and mirrors! I must be seriously insane!" I confess hysterically.

"Are you more afraid of the symptoms or what the symptoms may signify?" Doreen perceptively inquires.

"Both," I concede.

"You're not insane." Doreen casually states. "Your fear of the unknown is understandable and rational. Who do you see reflected besides yourself in glass and the mirror?"

I stare at her and snap the plastic of the water bottle in and out. The bottle crackles, crackles. Doreen tilts her head indicating that I should make eye contact. I make eye contact but I can't think of an answer. I'm actually surprised that I never considered prior to Doreen's question who appeared in the glass and mirror with me. I shrug.

"You don't know?" Doreen asks.

"I don't know," I admit.

"Now we're getting somewhere," Doreen exclaimed.

"Great," I respond sarcastically.

"Describe what happens when the shadow appears," she instructs.

"I can't really describe her/him/it because I never see any identifying features. At best, I see a shadow of someone behind me and her/his/its outline is similar to my own."

"Does anything occur prior to the shadow's appearance?" Doreen asked.

"No," I respond too quickly. Doreen says nothing but slightly tilts her head to the side as if trying to hear a whisper.

"What?" I ask. She says nothing and continues to look at me. I hear the clock ticking in our silence. I gaze out the window and watch the tree swaying slightly in the breeze. Who am I kidding? I'm avoiding the question.

"I'm avoiding the question," I admit.

"Let me rephrase it." Doreen asks, "what, if anything, precludes the appearance of the shadow in the mirror?"

In essence this question is the same as the prior question.

"Ah," I hesitate and add quickly, "I hear a strange whizzing sound followed by a noise that feels like equalizing ear pressure."

"And?" she asks. I hate those 'and' questions because I feel pressured to produce the balance of the answer.

"Help me," I ask honestly.

"I'd be happy to help you," Doreen responds. "You've done good work here today so I don't mind filling in the blanks, so to speak."

This time I'm the one tilting my head as I

adjust my posture on the couch as if waiting to hear an intriguing story. Doreen's response shocks me.

"The strange sound and equalizing of ear pressure is what happens when you 'disappear'."

"So," I begin cautiously, "if I disappear, the alter appears?"

Doreen merely nods slowly and adds, "This is the switch from one personality to the other."

"Why? Why do I need an alter?" I rasp.

"The question about why you 'need' an alter vs. why you 'have' an alter is an astute question." Doreen acknowledges.

I feel smart and proud and perk up a little. "How so?"

Doreen said that the subconscious mind creates an alter to protect or serve the original person when a trauma occurs usually in early childhood. Therefore, the original person actually 'needs' the alter to survive. The alter lives alternatively with the original person and in some cases has a separate distinct personality.

I speculate about my alter based on what Doreen has described and suddenly I feel like I'm on that familiar edge of the abyss ready to fall into the unknown. I can't resist the dizzying, spinning disorientation and disappear.

Session VIII

"I'm afraid to ask," I lament.

"I bet," Doreen acknowledges and adds, "Be brave, Kay. Ask."

"How long have I been gone?" I squeak.

"Too long," she laughs. "I missed you."

"Was the alter here?" I bravely inquire.

"Yes," Doreen admits.

I swallow hard but I have no saliva and expel a dry hacking cough. I cover my face with my hands.

"Disappearing again?" Doreen laughs.

"I'm scared," I confess putting my hands back onto my lap.

"Of what?" she asks.

"Did you meet the alter?" I ask bravely.

"Yes," she confirms and adds, "Would you like information about her?"

"Yes. No." I stammer and stare out the window. Doreen waits.

"Which is it; yes or no?" she patiently asks.

"Yes," I whisper as I lean closer to her rocking chair.

Doreen explains that the alter introduced herself as fifteen year old Ginger and while she and I seem to be a lot alike, Ginger appears to be fearless! Doreen describes Ginger as a risk taker, spontaneous and independent. Ginger doesn't hide or disappear. It's ironic that while I disappear, Ginger appears!

"What does she talk about?" I inquire.

"The life you share with her," Doreen says.

"How can we share a life?" I yell. "I didn't even know she existed until three minutes ago! I clap my hands rhythmically with each word as if to punctuate the obvious.

"Regardless of how you perceive the situation, Ginger does, in fact share your life. Her time line is continuous."

"Maybe I'm *her* alter," I hissed venomously. "Maybe I'm not the real person!" I jump off the couch and reach for the doorknob. I'm surprised Doreen hasn't moved or said anything to deter me so I run out of the office with the intent to retreat down the hall to my room.

I suddenly stop about fifteen feet from her office. I turn around and Doreen is standing by the open door looking at me. Once again, she tilts her head. I shrug my shoulders and turn around and walk back into the office. Doreen shuts the door behind us and says, "Good choice." She sits on the couch next to me.

"I hate Ginger," I confess surprised that I have recognized and expressed a spontaneous feeling.

"I think I'm jealous," I add and realize that I have identified a second feeling.

"Why 'jealous'?" Doreen asks.

I think a few moments and realize that I'm jealous because Ginger's life has continuity and mine doesn't. I don't understand how Ginger can be living my life when I don't. The statement sounds insane.

"Actually," Doreen explains as if she's read my thoughts, "Ginger is *you* but not fearful like you."

I exhale, scratch the top of my head and exhale again. Suddenly, something occurs to me and I'm urgently animated. "Did Ginger assault my boss?"

"No," Doreen replies.

"I don't remember assaulting my boss, so if Ginger didn't do it, who did?" As soon as I asked the question, the reply, although unprovoked, popped into my head. I was horrified and my hand flew over my mouth.

"Yes?" Doreen probes.

"There's *another*, isn't there?" I whisper.

"Yes," Doreen responds gently patting my forearm as I scream and collapse into a ball on the sofa.

The Assault

I'm incredulous about how vacation photos appear in my cubicle at work when I can't remember the vacation in which the photos were supposedly taken. One photo is of me on a ski slope appearing somewhat comfortable and confident as if I can snow ski. Another photo is of me in scuba diving gear with a big smile on my face at some Caribbean locale. I hold and scan the photo frames tenderly like they're a relic of my life.

"Don't you ever vacation with friends or family?" my co-worker asks. The truth is that I cannot recall but I respond cleverly,

"Who do you think is taking the picture?" I have no idea who took the photos.

Oddly enough, I'm familiar with the different stacks and trays that represent varying stages of work related tasks. I assume that when I'm working I'm in some kind of efficient and productive 'zone'. The work gets done somehow, although, I have no idea how. My co-workers think I'm shy because I don't talk much but that's because there are weeks that I cannot remember the office chit chat about upcoming weddings, baby showers, parties and who's doing who. I think it's interesting however that I (or one of the alters) attend some office social events but have no recollection. I politely say, "Thank you," when my office mate compliments my outfit for a specific event although I have no idea what I wore. When I review the photos of me at that function I speculate about the choice of clothing and accessories.

They're not what I would choose. I'm somewhat conservative (I think) while the woman in the picture representing me wears spiked shoes, dangling earrings and colorful, although not coordinated colors. I just shrug.

I don't recall in the first person how "I" or the other alter assaulted my boss. (Just saying the "other alter" makes me want to vomit. Thinking of myself in two or more people flat out makes me physically ill. Doreen says that becoming physically ill regarding the alters, mitigates or reduces the mental illness. Her theory is something about "you can't fix what you don't acknowledge.") Apparently my female boss commented publically about how absent-minded I was. She accused me of being an idiot savant because I was socially awkward but produced meticulous work. I learned from Doreen that the alter who bashed my boss in the head with a printer paper tray was Judy. Judy first appeared to me as a finger friend when I was about three years old. Most three year olds don't recognize conversational sarcasm Doreen explained. "Judy" didn't know how to interpret the bosses' smile with the sarcastic words combined with having a serious problem with female authority figures impulsively used the paper tray to act out with adult force. Judy, being a three year old in an adult body, ran screaming from the pod of cubicles down the hall into the restroom where the police found her sobbing uncontrollably behind a locked toilet stall sitting on the floor. The police kicked the door in, grabbed, arrested Judy and took her to jail. Consistent with a three year old behavior, Judy kept screaming that "Kay did it" and not her. The police weren't fazed having become accustomed to all types of criminals, drug addicts and crazies. The female boss while apologetic about her comments didn't think the situation warranted 22 stitches on the top of her head so she fired me (or Judy) and pressed charges.

Incredibly, I became aware of me, Kay, while sitting in a jail cell waiting to appear before the judge. I was terrified having no knowledge of what I had done or what had occurred to result in my detainment. Had I killed someone? Did I become a prostitute? Did I sell or ingest drugs? I was actually relieved when I heard the formal charges at the hearing that I had assaulted my boss. Hitting her in the head with a paper tray, while reprehensible, was less worrisome than murder, tricking or drug dealing. I recall smiling ever so slightly with gratitude at that last thought in which the judge determined to be an inappropriate response. Thankfully and ironically, I had mentally decompensated to such an extent that the judge ordered a psychiatric evaluation prior to court proceeding continuance.

"Yes," Doreen responded. "That's the gist of it. And I was assigned to your case."

"The rest is history," I claim as a bad joke. I tenderly think about Judy and Ginger and wonder about the life they've lived trying to protect me. At least I know or knew Judy because she was one of my finger friends in addition to Licky before mother found me a real flesh and blood friend. I have fond memories of Judy and how loyal and comforting she was. I recall how I thought she was almost magical and dependable, appearing just when I needed her.

The other alter's existence surprised me. Although I can somewhat rationalize how Ginger has served me, it's difficult to think how "she" has been lurking somewhere unbeknownst to me. Truthfully, it's unnerving.

"Lurking is a sinister word," Doreen observes.

"Does Ginger lurk?" I ask.

"She watches out for you and intervenes when you, Kay, don't have the social or mental skills to cope." She explains.

"So, instead of Ginger being a 'lurker', she's an 'intervener'," I cleverly state.

"What does an 'intervener' do," Doreen asks.

I have no clue what an 'intervener' does and now I'm sorry that I mentioned it. The longer I think about it; however, I determine that Ginger saves me from becoming more emotionally unraveled than I am and helps me to live a productive life even if I have no recollection. Calling Ginger a 'savior' seems sacrilegious in my mind but I can't think of a more descriptive word.

"Ginger is my savior," I claim and add, "in a non religious way, of course."

"Of course," Doreen acknowledges.

We both sit comfortably silent like we're
each lost in our respective thoughts. I'm reflective
of how I began the journey to mental health with
Doreen and appreciate how far I've come. As if
she's read those thoughts, she says, "You may
celebrate your progression but don't get smug on
me!" She smiles.

"Oh, God, "I groan. "What do you want to
explore now?"

"We're avoiding your mother's mental
health issues and the appearance of Judy as a viable
alter." Doreen states. I nod. She's mentioned
before that she thinks that my mother had mental
health issues. I remember her saying it more than
once during our sessions. Questioning the
appearance of Judy surprises me because I'm

conscious about when I created her and when she appeared. I ponder the word 'viable' and question Doreen about what it means.

"There's a specific time in which Judy becomes autonomous meaning that you don't manifest her when you want to. As a child, you would call on her and she would be available to you. At some point, you didn't need to call on her. She appeared on her own volition."

"Oh, God," I groan again and suddenly blurt, "Maybe the two issues are related to each other!"

"Yes?" Doreen probes. I shrug, "I don't know." And shake my head.

"We'll see," she says gently opening the

door to her office. My time in session has come to

an end.

Mother Disappears

It's a warm and sunshiny spring day as I
recall playing with my new 'real' friend, Ellen, in
the side yard between our houses. Her mother, Pat
is sitting on the porch stoop reading the newspaper
and watching us play. She occasionally looks up at
us to see what we're doing. We're playing house in
a cardboard box that has words printed on the side.
We have our dollies and blankets and we're talking
about house play using our toddler vocabulary. The
phone rings inside Ellen's house and Pat runs inside
to answer it. I hear her voice but can't hear the
specifics about the conversation other than when
Pat laughs near the end. She returns to the yard and

resumes reading the newspaper. Suddenly and without provocation, Ellen slaps me on the head with an open hand and yells, "No!" I'm shocked because she has never hit me before. I look up at Pat while rubbing the top of my head and she says, "Work it out." I wanted her to intervene but she didn't. I pull Ellen's hair and she screamed like her skin has been pulled off her body. "Kay!" Pat yells as she jumps off the stoop, runs to her sweet little girl and scoops her up into her arms. "That's not nice!" Pat admonishes me as I grab my doll and blanket and walk back across the grass to my house. I look over my shoulder as Pat and her daughter have gone inside their house. I open the screen door and go inside to the kitchen and sit under the table and continue to play house. I don't know how long I played but I became hungry and it occurred to me that I hadn't seen my mother since I went out to play with Ellen.

"Mommy?" I called out as I crawled out from under the kitchen table and walked into the living room. The t.v. was off. It was beginning to become dark outside so I climbed onto the couch and turned on the lamp. "Mommy?" I called out again as I sat on

the couch momentarily scanning the inside of the house. I could see down the hallway and I noticed that my parent's bedroom door was closed. Dad was working in the oil field and wasn't home. Sometimes when my dad was home from work and I went out to play with Ellen, the bedroom door was closed. I was told that mommy and daddy wanted 'privacy'. I was confused about the door being shut now because Dad wasn't home.

"Why is the door closed?" I wondered. Maybe my mother was napping. I jumped off the couch and returned to the kitchen. The refrigerator door was too heavy for me to open so I pulled out two drawers in the kitchen cabinet and climbed up onto the counter. I stood up and looked into the cabinet and saw a jar of peanut butter and a box of crackers. I took them off the shelf and set them onto the counter as I climbed down on the drawers. Once back onto the floor, I could not reach the peanut butter and crackers so I climbed back onto the countertop. The peanut butter jar lid was too tight to open but the crackers were easy to unwrap so I ate a lot of them. I became thirsty so I crawled along the counter until I reached the sink where there was a clean cup. I turned the water knob and water poured into and over the top of the cup. I turned the knob and the water went off. The cup was very full so I just slurped at the very top so not to spill. After I was done drinking, I sat on the counter for a little longer. I became distressed as the telephone began to ring and continued to ring and ring and ring. Mother didn't answer it and I couldn't climb down from the counter fast enough to get to it before it stopped. I crawled back along the counter top and climbed down the two drawers onto the kitchen floor. I ran very quickly to the phone stand.

The telephone sat on a small stand in the hallway under a mirror between my and my parent's bedrooms. I sat down on the floor near the telephone in case it rang again I could answer it right away.

"Did it ring again?" Doreen asked leaning

forward in her rocking chair. She appeared to be stretching out her back.

"I don't know because I think I fell asleep on the floor in the hallway," I recalled.

"Let's assume that you did fall asleep on the floor. What's the next thing you remember?" she asked.

I thought for a moment and considered the question. "About that subject specifically?" I ask qualifying my response or perhaps hedging the question.

"No. In general. What do you remember after that?"

Once again, the response is slow immerging into my consciousness. Unconnected pale colored images float up to my consciousness and quickly dissipate. The tree outside of Doreen's window catches my attention as it usually does although I'm no longer entranced. The tree is just a tree outside of the window responding to nature. Suddenly, without prompting or any rationale, a thought pops into my head.

I gasp in consideration of my answer.

"What?" Doreen asks.

"Oh my God," I respond. "The next thing I recall is being in my grandparent's kitchen for supper."

"Like the dream?" She asks.

I slowly nod.

"Do you have any idea how much time elapsed between the telephone ringing and you being aware of grandparent's kitchen?" Doreen asks.

"No," I admit. "No." I state again.

It seems like minutes before I'm brave enough to

ask, "Does Ginger or Judy know?"

"Yes", Doreen admits. "Judy knows. Would you like to know?"

"Do I want to know?" I rhetorically ask her.

"How do you feel when you're in your grandparent's kitchen?" she asks.

"Safe," I reply.

"It's reasonable to think that you're safe despite whatever happened between the phone ringing and you remembering being in the kitchen. You're safe now, too." She affirmed.

"O.k.," I give my permission to hear Judy's story of the time lapse. "Wait! Is it a scary story?"

"It would be scary story for a small child," Doreen confirms and then adds as an afterthought, "the memory of the event will not destroy you. You will not 'splinter' now into another person.

Actually, knowing the truth could be very

therapeutic."

"O.k." I say not too confidently. I grab a

pillow from the couch and hold it close to my chest

as if to deflect whatever is coming from piercing

my heart and ripping my very soul to shreds.

Doreen recalled what Judy had told her in a

previous session about the telephone ringing.

Kay/Judy did fall asleep on the floor in the hallway

but Judy heard the phone ringing and woke to

answer it.

"Hello?" Judy asked.

"It's grandmother, honey. May I speak to

your mother?"

"I don't know where she is."

"What? What do you mean? Is she in the

bathroom?"

"No."

"Did she make dinner?"

"No."

"What did you eat?"

"Crackers."

"Is mommy in the bedroom?"

"I don't know. The door is shut and daddy isn't home."

"Stay right there, Kay. I'm coming over."

Grandmother hung up the telephone and so did Judy. But Judy didn't stay 'right there' as grandmother ordered. Judy needed to go potty so went into the bathroom. When she flicked the light on, Judy noticed that there was red stuff in the toilet bowl. It didn't disturb her because she thought it looked like chunky red punch drink. Judy toileted and cleaned herself and walked back to sit near the phone to wait for grandmother.

"Should I ask or wait?" I asked Doreen.

"It depends." She responded.

"On what?" I asked.

"If you really want an answer or if you're just curious. Curiosity killed the cat, you know." Doreen added, "That's bad humor. I apologize."

"I need an answer," I responded, "but, I'm also curious."

Doreen continued that grandmother came over to the house and found Kay/Judy sitting in the hallway. She picked up her granddaughter and took her to the living room and placed her into an easy chair. "Wait here," grandmother instructed. Kay/Judy saw grandmother walk down the hall turning on lights as she went. She knocked on the bedroom door. "Peggy," grandmother called.

"Peggy, I'm coming in." Kay/Judy saw the light go on in her parent's bedroom and then heard grandmother say again, "Peggy, Peggy. Please wake up, honey." And then Kay/Judy heard their sweet grandmother scream and scream. Grandmother, bent over with a hand to her mouth, ran quickly from the bedroom into the bathroom and began screaming again. Judy had not flushed the toilet and Grandmother knew exactly what the 'chunky red punch' was.

"What was it?" I whispered interrupting the story.

"The best that the authorities could put together at that time was that your mother had spontaneously aborted into the toilet during the first trimester of her pregnancy." Doreen gently said. I considered what Doreen revealed and a thought occurred to me.

"She was dead in the bedroom wasn't she?" I cried. "My mommy was dead, wasn't she?" Tears began pouring down my cheeks.

"Yes, Kay," Doreen said softly. "Yes, your mother was dead." Doreen handed me the box of tissues and sat down next to me on the sofa. She tenderly patted my arm.

When I had recovered from the sobbing and hiccoughing, I asked if my mother had bled to death from the miscarriage.

"No," Doreen said.

"How did she die?" I asked quietly. I had to know.

"She died from a drug overdose." She stated. Doreen waited for my reaction but somehow I wasn't shocked.

"How?" I stammered.

"Autopsies back in those days were not as sophisticated or revealing as they are today. The best that the medical examiner could determine was that she died from an overdose of phenobarbital and alcohol. Your mother was still living when the fetus was expelled. Your grandmother observed blood in your parent's bed which indicates she continued to bleed before succumbing to the overdose."

"My poor crazy mother," was all I could think of to say as I was too stunned to say anything else. Suicides were shameful during the 1950s and were not openly spoken about. While having miscarriages during that decade was more socially acceptable, women's issues weren't. No one ever spoke about what happened to my mother but as a small child I realized that she had disappeared into a wooden box and I never saw her again. Part of me was happy that the bad mother was gone and would never come back but as the days and weeks went on, I missed the good mother and wondered what happened to her. I thought I was the cause of my mother's disappearance. I was to blame because I didn't knock on the bedroom door. I quickly brushed the thought aside.

"My next memory is being in my grandparents' kitchen," I offered before Doreen could ask. "I stayed at their house while my dad and the Heider's made the 'arrangements'. I slept with my grandmother and grandfather for a while but then they decorated the front bedroom for me and I slept there. I never went back to my parents' house. Dad would stay with me at the Heiders when he was in town. But now that I'm thinking about it, I lost my mother, my house and my bedroom in a very short time. That's a significant amount of loss for a child."

"Wisely spoken," Doreen affirmed. "Do you recall your mother's funeral?" she asked.

"I recall more imagery than anything else; not specific memories. I recall the cotton from the cottonwood trees looking like snow blowing at the cemetery. I brush them out of my face. The sun is bright as I shield my eyes with my hand. As always, my shoes are very uncomfortable. My dress is itchy and I scratch my elbows and knees. My dad's hand gently covers mine as if to say, "Stop it."

I'm sitting in a chair next to dad and the rest of the family in front of my mother's box. I recall wanting to open it to see if she was really inside because I was afraid that the bad mother might want to trick me. My dad said that it wasn't a good idea to look into the box because mother was 'dead'. I'm holding a small bouquet of yellow wildflowers and when dad tells me, I stand up and throw them onto the box but they don't stay and drop one by one into the hole. He puts three red roses on top of the box and pats it gently. He's crying and I hug his leg. It seems like everybody who was sitting in the chairs is crying. Boxes of tissues are passed back and forth between the sad people. I look around. It's such a nice day and all I want to do is go home, change my clothes and play.

"You've done a good job here," Doreen affirms. "You, as Kay were able to stay emotionally present during your mother's funeral service I think because you were familiar with funerals and the cemetery. You could cope."

"Why, then did Judy stay and why then did I create Ginger?" I asked.

"Judy stayed because of the imagery. As a child you were aware of the blood in the toilet, you heard words like 'suicide' and experienced your dad and families' grief but you couldn't understand the significance. Couple that with the significant changes that occurred to you after your mother's passing; going to live with your grandparents, new room, and learning different routines and it was too much."

"I wanted her dead," I confessed in a small voice.

"I know," Doreen admitted.

"What! You knew?!!" I yelled standing up

approaching her forcefully. She didn't flinch.

"That's it," Doreen reaffirmed. "It's a
natural feeling for a child to periodically hate or
want their parent/caregiver to die. A child doesn't
know what death is until they're about six to eight
years old. They don't understand that death is
irreversible and forever. You were only three years
old when you first acknowledged that you wanted
your mother to die not cognizant of the reality of
what that meant. Hating and being frightened of the
bad mother was normal for a child your age. For
you, the problem started when you couldn't depend
on your mother because she was unpredictable; one
day loving and nurturing and the next cold and off-
putting. You didn't know whether to come closer
or go away. Combine that with her taking drugs
and alcohol, a father who is gone for long stretches

of time and you've got a very toxic home life."

"I feel guilty," I confessed. "I hated her but in reality she was a sick puppy."

"You didn't know that then," Doreen stated. "You couldn't have. Your dad didn't know. Your grandmother didn't know. How were you supposed to know?"

I shrugged.

Symmetry

I don't have the dream of my grandparent
Heider's kitchen as often as I used to. Doreen said
it was because I felt safer in my conscious living
and don't need the reassuring safety of the dream.
I've come to accept Ginger and Judy as part of me
and in addition, I've tried to understand the best
parts about them. Doreen says it will take a while
before I'm fully integrated but in the meantime, I'm
living those annoying two hour increments.

Symmetry still scares me but I think Doreen
and I are onto something. The grandparents
Heiders lived on Aurora Street and they're buried
about a mile down that same street where my
mother is also buried. The Heiders being buried on

Aurora Street means that, of course they died and are interred there. The dream begins as I slam the screen door of the front porch and walk down the concrete sidewalks buckled by the roots of old cottonwood trees. I walk, passing familiar sites until I get to the cemetery and arrive at the double headstone joined by a flowerpot. I read their names, "Grant and Juanita" along with requisite birth and death dates. The headstone also memorializes their wedding anniversary date and the enjoining flowerpot is inscribed with "Heider". There's an addition to the family plot in this dream. Next to the Heider double headstone is fresher single marker in which I now stand taller. It reads:

"Peggy Heider Smith: Daughter. Wife. Mother 1931-1955 Rest in Peace."

Acknowledgements

I would like to acknowledge and thank the following people who supported, encouraged and worked diligently to make this book come to fruition:

Thank you to my copy editor, Tiffany Avans. I appreciate the time and effort she put into editing the text. This was a difficult and challenging book to edit because of the intertwining story line.

Thank you to my friend of over 40 years, Pamala (Pam Pam) Barbosa. She said it could be written and she was right.

I'm appreciative of my husband John who after 43 years of marriage knows me better than anyone and continues to love me.

My son, Ryan inspired me to write my own book instead of editing other people's work.

And last but not least, I'm grateful to my daughter, Amy (Jenae) who understood and encouraged my dream to publish.

This is a work of fiction but as in any work of fiction, there are facets of truth. Doreen by another name exists. I am eternally grateful for her brilliance as a therapist and friend. I have known Ginger since I was three years old and the friendship continues. Ginger has lived an interesting life (to say the least) and continues to inspire. Of course my parents and grandparents existed. They have all gone to their heavenly home. It's true that my maternal grandparents are buried on the end of the street in which they lived: Aurora Street in Fort Morgan, Colorado.

About the Author

This is Karla Williams Noonan's first book although she was first published 49 years ago when she was a reporter for her city's local newspaper. Karla wrote a regular and reoccurring column in which she described issues of interest to the teens of the late 1960's and early 1970's. Karla continued to write for her college newspaper as she pursued a degree in Journalism.

Life intervened with a wedding, children

and a second career in education where Karla was a successful grant and curriculum writer. Upon retirement, Karla decided to continue to write and finish the book that had been in the works for six years. That book is Aurora Street.

Karla has been married to John for 43 years. The couple has two children; Ryan who is married to Jessica and Amy who has a huge Cane Corso dog named Ceto. John and Karla's household is complete with a cat named Abby and a dog, Morgan.

Karla spends her summers on Lake Alcova in Wyoming enjoining wide open spaces.